FINDING WAYS

by
Patricia McGrane

McGrane, Patricia
Finding Ways: a novel/Patricia McGrane
ISBN: 978-0-9991094-4-1

Credits

Interior design and Cover design by Ryan Salinetti, Breakwater Design, LLC (bwdandc.com)

Printed by IngramSpark, Nashville, Tennessee

patriciamcgrane.com

PREFACE

For many fiction writers, myself included, the basis for a story is a small incident in the past which dwells in the far reaches of memory until the time is right to bring it forward to let it flourish through research and imagination into a creation all its own. Set in the early 1970's, **Finding Ways** is that type of fictional story. Its setting is in the early 1970's. All the characters, settings and situations are imaginary, but the idea for this book grew out of a minor experience my husband and I had in the 1970's when we rented an old house without knowing a commune had taken over two houses down the block from us.

We stayed in the house for about eighteen months and during that time we mostly remained observers to the commune activities. However, the unusual troubling, seeds of memory remained and grew into **Finding Ways**.

Patricia McGeane

Melbourne Beach, Florida, 2025

"The World is so unpredictable. Things happen suddenly, unexpectedly. We want to feel we are in control of our own existence. In some ways we are, in some ways we're not. We are ruled by the forces of chance and coincidence."

—Paul Auster

()

Chapter 1

In the early 1970's, Ways, a Massachusetts based commune which traced its early beginnings as far back as early colonial days, adopted a new master plan. It called for its young charismatic apostles known as Fathers to fan out across the United States to research small college or university towns that could be of future interest. Their mission was to establish and grow new branches of Ways. Over the years, Ways had become a haven for low and middle income lost souls, as well as wealthy, but disillusioned, traditional church goers. All were seeking the culture of a do-it-yourself type of religion that encouraged members to interpret scriptures in the Bible as they saw fit, not on the accepted denominational guidelines. In addition, Ways offered instant community with a free place to live, free food, open sexual relations and a type of mutual belonging never experienced before.

Father Michael Brown was one of these apostles. Tall with dark hair, an athletic build, and a charming demeanor, he was chosen to explore the Southeast. Because of its reputation for strong Bible Belt preachers and congregations, the region had already been identified as fertile ground for potential Ways expansion.

When he found Beecher University in quiet, genteel Oakton,

Tennessee, he notified the Elders at Ways that he was certain he had located a new site for the commune expansion plan. They in turn wired him funds to purchase a property that was big enough, not only to house multiple new members and families, but also to accommodate large congregational meetings.

Father Michael realized that many potential new members could be students or local down-on-their luck townies who didn't own cars. With that in mind, he began exploring available real estate properties within walking distance of the University and the downtown Oakton area. He soon found the town had many large older homes, some of which pre-dated the Civil War. Many of the properties had been sub-divided with newer ranch-style houses built on small lots. Others still retained several acres of surrounding land with barns and outbuildings still standing. He quickly minimized his search for this last type of setting—a big old house with surrounding land and extra buildings. The house at the end of Sutter Court seemed to fit the new commune's needs perfectly, but it was for rent not for sale.

Dressed in a white oxford cloth shirt, khaki pants, a blue blazer and cordovan loafers, he went to the real estate office and introduced himself as Michael Brown, a business man from Boston. When he inquired about the Sutter Court property, Mark Green, the real estate agent sighed and shook his head. "Martha Sutter will never sell and if she ever does rent it, she and her niece want to continue living in a portion of the house while it's rented. It's been on the market for a long time and you can understand why. No one wants to share the house with them."

"I still want to look at the house and stroll the property.

Maybe I can talk her into some sort of agreeable arrangement," Father Michael said.

Mark shrugged. "I'll call them now and see if we can look at the house, but the talking thing is a different matter. Miss Sutter is a deaf mute. Her niece will have to interpret for you with the sign language. You still interested?"

Father Michael nodded. "Make the appointment. I want this property."

()

chapter 2

From a distance, the Sutter mansion appeared to be a stately two story gray clapboard home with double hung windows and a portico sheltering the front door. But as Father Michael and Mark Green neared the house and drove up the steep rocky driveway, it became obvious that years of neglect had taken its toll. The gray color was actually faded white chipped paint, exposing the dirty wooden boards and the roof was missing many of the shingles. The windows were surprisingly intact, but the glass panes had turned a honey color. Collapsed downspouts and gutters littered the lawn.

Mark shook his head. "What a mess! I haven't been up here in a while. You still want to look inside?"

Michael looked around the yard and nodded. He could see the large barn peeking through the trees to the side of the house. "I'll need to see the inside and the whole property. That's why I'm here."

Mark opened the car door. "They're expecting us. Let's see what's happening inside." They walked past a little blue Rambler parked underneath the portico and up the steps to a worn oak door adorned with a Medusa head door knocker. "Charming," Mark mumbled as he pulled up the knocker and rapped on the door.

Unexpectedly, a narrow strip of Medusa 's face slid open slightly and a woman's voice quietly said, "Yes?"

Mark cleared his throat. "It's Mark Green, your realtor. I called earlier. This man is interested in renting the house."

The Medusa face closed, a latch turned, and a beautiful, fair-skinned, young woman with curly blonde hair and bright blue eyes opened the door. "Hello Mark, you haven't been here for a while," she greeted them with a smile.

Mark shook her hand. "It's good to see you Hope. This is Mr. Michael Brown. We'd like to take a look around. Is your aunt here?"

Hope laughed. "Of course, she's here. You know she doesn't leave the house. She's in her plant room. I'll let her know you're here. You go ahead and start looking around."

The two men stepped into a marble foyer with a crystal chandelier and a soaring curved staircase leading to the upstairs. On one side was a large dining room with a long mahogany table and chairs. Three tarnished silver candelabra with melted yellowed candles surrounded by piles of old wax were centered on the table. A country kitchen with a large sink, heavy gas stove and old fashioned refrigerator were located behind a swinging door. A pantry with floor to ceiling shelves and a small maid's bathroom were off to one side.

On the opposite side of the foyer was a Victorian style sitting room with ornately carved wooden back settees with faded rose colored velvet cushions. A threadbare Oriental rug graced the dark wood floors and a closed grand piano sat in one corner. Heavy gray brocade drapes hung over the windows blocking the sunlight.

French doors opened to a library with rolling ladders and shelves lined with books to the ceiling. More books were piled on the floor along with old magazines and newspapers. A twin bed was set up in the center of the room with a small table and lamp.

Neither man had said much while they were touring the rooms. "It's all overwhelming isn't it?" Mark finally commented. "Like being in another world."

Father Michael nodded. "It was clearly a very elegant home years ago, and the collection of books in this library is magnificent." He was paging through one of the books when Hope found them.

"Aunt Martha will see you," she said, opening another set of French doors at the far end of the library.

Martha Sutter's plant room was no small greenhouse. Instead it was a soaring solarium which extended across the back of the entire first floor. "Wait until you see this room," Mark said in a low voice. "She spends all of her money keeping it in perfect condition. The air circulation and irrigation systems are state of the art. Never mind that the rest of the old place is in serious disrepair!"

An elderly white haired woman was seated in a high-back wheelchair amidst the tall trees and lush flowering plants. Giant green fern fronds trailed over her shoulders enveloping her. She was dressed in a high-neck black dress with a long pearl and diamond necklace around her neck. A white lace shawl cloaked her shoulders under the ferns.

"Aunt Martha, you know Mark Green and this is Michael Brown. He's interested in renting the house," Hope signed and said.

Martha extended her thin wrinkled hands. Diamond and emerald rings sparkled on her gnarled fingers which tightly gripped both men's hands at the same time. For a moment, neither man spoke. The vision of this glittering old woman in the opulent, exotic tropical setting, all within the rundown mansion was too eerily surreal.

Finally, Father Michael recovered and pulled his hand away. "Your home is beautiful and very interesting. I'd like to look through the upstairs and then walk the grounds. Would you mind if I take some pictures while I'm here? It will help me in thinking about an offer."

After Hope signed his words, Martha stared at Michael with piercing eyes and then waved her hand wide. She wheeled her chair away from them, deeper back into the plants that shielded her face. "She means you're free to look around and take pictures," Hope said in a low voice.

"Tell her thank you. We'll let you know when we're leaving," Mark said, as he and Father Michael backed away and left the solarium.

The upstairs had four minimally furnished bedrooms and two working bathrooms. Only the master bedroom and bath appeared to be in use, while the others had dirty dust covers over the furniture. Many candles of different sizes and shapes along with matches were in every room. "Makes you wonder about the electrical power on this floor, doesn't it?" Mark observed.

Father Michael didn't answer. He was at the end of the center hallway staring out the window into the back yard. "Looks like there's a cemetery back here. It's all overgrown, but I can see some headstones and a mausoleum. Did you know about this?"

Mark nodded. "It's an old family graveyard. It's no longer

in use, but that's another reason this property won't sell."

"What's that way beyond the cemetery and the trees where the property drops off?" Father Michael pointed.

"That's the Broadway Market and Drug Store. It was built in the 1950's when old Mr. Sutter, Martha's father, sold off that parcel of land. Originally the Sutter property extended all the way to the river, about ten miles beyond the Market. Mr. Sutter divided that land into residential lots and called the neighborhood Sutterwood On The River.

Father Michael smiled. "This is my kind of property. It's an intriguing place with mysterious women and a never ending story. I like that. Let's look around outside."

Mark frowned. "You can't be seriously thinking of taking this place? I can show you several other properties which would be in better condition and not so strange and burdensome."

Father Michael opened the front door. "I like this one and I think the Sutter ladies are interesting, not burdensome."

Outside, the late afternoon sky had turned gray and misty with wisps of fog and occasional shards of sun. The men trudged through the waist high weeds to the barn and pulled open the doors. Dim light trickled through between the wooden slats. Old rusted farm equipment and a 1950's Cadillac filled the space. Tools were piled high in the stalls except for one which held an old buggy with velvet cushions and a jump seat on the back. A light bulb dangled from the ceiling.

Mark whistled. "Wow! I've never looked in here. If you could clean this stuff up and get it working, you could sell it for a lot of money. Some collectors would pay a fortune for these vintage pieces."

Father Michael was inspecting the wiring and the plumbing. He was secretly thrilled with the surprisingly good condition of the big barn. He imagined it accommodating large groups of people for commune services. The money from the sale of the large collection of vintage items would help finance the needed updating and renovating. But all he finally said to Mark was, "It's good there's usable electrical wiring and plumbing in here."

The other two story outbuildings were so filled with old furniture, wooden crates and steamer trunks, the men could barely force the doors open, let alone walk inside. The structures appeared to have been either living quarters or workshops at some point in time. Again, the good news for Father Michael was that both buildings appeared to be wired for electricity and had water pipes and possibly bathrooms.

Back under the portico, Father Michael and Mark discussed the rental fees and the sharing of the house with the Sutter women. "I can go along with Miss Sutter continuing to live in the library and solarium, and Hope occupying the upstairs bedroom if she wants to. I suppose she'll need to continue to use the kitchen too. We'll have to work out that arrangement. I'll agree to rent and occupy the rest of the house, the barn and outbuildings. And as part of my rental fee, I'll provide landscaping and maintenance for the entire property. I'm offering $300 in monthly rent with the immediate option to buy the property if or when they want to sell."

Mark nodded. "The standard lease will require two months' rent in advance. Otherwise that's a solid offer. But this place needs so much updating, how are you going to do all the work and maintenance yourself?"

Father Michael smiled. "I'm a family counselor and I have a large network of associates and friends. They're all good workers and talented tradesmen. They like challenges, just as I do. Restoration of mind, soul and property is what we do. After we get the property in order, I'd like to set up my practice here. Please make the offer just as I outlined."

Martha Sutter's quick agreement to the terms of the rental proposal was a surprise to Hope and Mark, but not to Father Michael. He just smiled and took her hand. "Tell her we will make this arrangement work. I'll move in next month and get started," he said to Hope, who signed his words.

Martha smiled up at him and signed, "I knew one day you would come back."

Hope frowned when she interpreted those words. "I don't know what she means about you coming back. She must have you confused with someone else. "

But Father Michael patted his heart and squeezed Martha's hand. "I think I know what she means and I will make her happy." "Unbelievable!" Mark laughed and shook hands with everyone. "Congratulations to all. I'll prepare the lease."

Father Michael handed the camera to Mark and asked if he would take a picture of him with Martha and Hope before they left. The women agreed, but only Hope looked at the camera. Martha turned her head away at the last minute and then backed into the ferns.

◯

chapter 3

Ways' Boston, Massachusetts office was in a two story stone building on a narrow side street off The Commons. The small sign on the door simply said The Foundation. The entry level consisted of a reception desk, a waiting room and two small offices. From time to time, the head Elders and accountants used the offices. Upstairs was a small kitchen and a large conference room.

Miles away from Ways large farm commune in the Berkshire Mountains, the Boston office was used to conduct business meetings, oversee the expansion plans, and control the financial side of the organization. All the monetary gifts and tithes to Ways and the surrendering of assets and valuables from new members passed through this office before being banked or sold. Proceeds were then deposited in various small inconspicuous accounts. Newly established communes received monthly monetary support as needed until they became self-sufficient.

Today Father Michael was meeting with the head Elder, Bishop John, and two other Elders who served on the Planning Board, overseeing the apostolic expansion. He had arrived early to prepare his presentation of the Sutter property. He filled the large law table with more than one hundred photos of the land, the main house, the barn and outbuildings. He had enlarged the final picture of Martha and Hope Sutter.

When Bishop John and the other two Elders, Brother Phillip and Brother Paul, arrived, they spent more than an hour studying the display and asking questions about the condition of all the buildings. Father Michael outlined his plan for cleaning up the main house and barn right away. "We should be able to hold meetings there within a few months, if you can spare me a team of workers. I'll recruit new Ways members as fast as I can from the University and the surrounding area. There's a large population of affluent well educated people there. They already tend to lean toward socialistic views for the betterment of the world. Ways offers them an opportunity to openly embrace socialism and practice it."

"What about the lower income people and the Black population?" Bishop John asked.

Father Michael nodded. "There's a fairly large, predominantly Black neighborhood near the downtown area of Oakton. Not too long ago, it was a completely segregated area. A couple of Black churches and what used to be a school are still there. A few poor whites live there, but quite a few more live in ramshackle houses on the outskirts of town. That's where a lot of charismatic preaching activity goes on."

"Do you think you can tap into those two areas and pull members over to Ways?" Brother Paul asked.

"A number of these people are disadvantaged in some way which makes them well suited for a communal way of life. They're a mix of winos, drug addicts, a few disabled veterans and even a few ex-convicts. None of them are permanently employed. If they try to work at all, they rely on day jobs and then use food banks to get by. They seem lost and not particularly motivated to try to rise above their situations. Ways' offer of spiritual support, a free place to live and free food in exchange for becoming working commune members will be very attractive. And that, of course, will enable us to control their emotional behavior and essentially their whole lives."

"I agree with everything you're describing," Brother Phillip said. "But the hardest part will be controlling how they spend their time, if any, outside Ways, and knowing who their potentially influential sources of information are outside the commune. Once you convince them to join us, you have to limit their contact with other family members and outsiders."

Father Michael shrugged. "You're right of course, but there's so much work to be done on the property, I can keep them busy all day and night. There won't be much time for family or friends outside Ways."

Bishop John tapped the picture of Martha and Hope Sutter with his forefinger. "What about these Sutter women? Your plan is to eventually buy their property, but for now, they still own it and you've agreed they can continue to live there with you. It all seems very awkward and risky for our mission. You don't foresee them as a problem?"

Father Michael grinned. "Not at all. They're our assets. The older woman Martha seemed taken with me right away. Besides being deaf and mute, she doesn't appear mentally stable. She keeps telling me, 'I knew you would come back.' I believe she thinks I'm someone from her past who is back in her life at last, and I'm happy to go along with her."

"How are you planning to convince them to sell you the property? That's key to our expansion plan," Bishop John pressed him.

"Hope is Martha's only heir. She was finishing high school around the time her parents died. Since then she has devoted her life to taking care of Martha. My plan is to marry Hope as soon as possible. Both her parents were deaf mutes too, so her upbringing was very unusual. She's never been exposed to traditional organized religion and had very little worldly experience. There've been no men in her life and she seems very gullible. It will be easy to convince her that I love her, and Ways is her salvation. After we're married, I'll enlist her help in persuading Martha to sign the property over to us because we're the future of the Sutter family."

Bishop John drummed his fingers on the table. "You've only been living there for a few weeks. If these women don't go along with your plans, then what?"

Father Michael sighed. "Then with Ways' blessing, I will help that crazy, old woman on her journey to her next life."

Bishop John exhaled. "You're certain you could do this ultimate service for Ways?"

Father Michael nodded and spoke quietly. "Of course, I hope it never comes to that, but yes, I would do it for Ways. The Sutter property will be ours."

◯

Chapter 4

Branch Monroe eased the Ryder rental truck up Sutter Court. The short, narrow, tree lined street was a mishmash of clapboard and brick houses, some neat and well-kept and others dilapidated tear-downs. All the structures were dwarfed by the towering, forlorn mansion high on the hill at the end of the street. It was early September, but the Southern mountain air already had a touch of fall, signaling the beginning of a new school year.

Branch parked in front of a small white house with a wrap-around porch near the end of the street. Thick woods separated the house from the old, antebellum house on the hill. His wife Livy with their two year-old daughter Rory followed behind in their Volkswagen Bug. "We made it honey," she whispered, looking at Rory asleep in the back seat. Then she watched Branch carefully climb down out of the truck cab. He limped toward her, slightly favoring his stiff left knee. He had injured it during a college football game years earlier and now arthritis had set in. He opened the VW door and kissed her. "Come on, let's look inside," he said, helping her out of the car and then reaching into the back seat to pick up Rory.

Holding hands, the couple walked through the wooden gate and climbed the low steps to the front porch. Double-beveled glass, floor to ceiling doors rose before them and a slatted wooden chair swing swayed on the side porch. "You're going to like it, I promise," Branch said smiling and handing her the door key.

The old fashioned key had a large round head and a wide, notched tooth that fit into the keyhole. "This looks like the key to my parents' house. I guess that's a good sign," Livy laughed as the latch clicked and one of the doors creaked open.

When they stepped inside, Livy gasped. The small foyer opened into a living room with a high ceiling and freshly painted cream colored walls combined with polished wood floors, a marble fireplace and wooden pocket doors. All spoke silently of a much earlier elegant life. "I never expected this, Branch," she said softly, as she ventured down the long center hallway, deeper into the house.

On one side of the hall was a large dining room with an ornate floral bas-relief ceiling, crystal chandelier and French doors that opened onto the circular porch. On the other side was a large bedroom complete with a window seat, walk-in closets, and a dressing room. Adjoining this room was an old fashioned bathroom with a marble sink, claw-footed bathtub and a high toilet with a wooden seat and ceramic flush handle.

The back of the house consisted of a large family kitchen with a wood floor, a farm sink, 1950's type appliances and a swinging door opening into the dining room. A glassed in sun porch extended behind the kitchen, overlooking a deep narrow backyard that ended in an alleyway. The partially finished basement contained a big coal furnace that had been converted to oil-forced air and modern hook-ups for a washer and dryer. Old chests and tools were scattered around the walls.

By the time they finished touring the house, Rory was awake and squirming in Branch's arms. He set her down and she took off down the hallway to explore the house on her own. The sound of her shoes clicking on the wood floors echoed through the empty house and her giggles bounced off the walls. Livy settled down on the window seat in the living room and kicked off her shoes. She relaxed against the windows, unclasped her long light brown hair and shook it loose to fall over her shoulders. Branch joined her and stretched out full length on the seat. He rested his head in her lap and closed his eyes. "So what do you think?" he asked.

Livy smiled and stroked his thick dark hair. "I love the elegant Victorian feeling. It's almost like we've stepped back in time. Tell me again how you found it."

"It was really just a coincidence. A rental notice was posted outside the graduate office where I registered. I had stopped by there to make sure they had received my GI Bill paperwork to cover the tuition. I took down the notice and asked the registrar for directions. It turned out the notice had just been posted that morning and Sutter Court is   only a few blocks from the campus. After I drove by here, I found a phone booth and called the owners to ask to look inside," Branch explained.

"And you said the owners live next door?"

"The Bakers. Yeah, they live right over there in that brick house," he said, pointing past the porch swing. "They seemed like a nice older couple and the house was a great find for us. So I gave them a deposit and signed a year's lease. I'll introduce you when they get home from work. The rent is only $185 a month. We should be able to live very comfortably especially after you find a job. Even if we don't like it, the MBA program only takes a year if I go straight through and then we'll be able to settle some place permanently."

Livy stood up. "We're going to be fine. The house is charming. It's freeing to be away from the military life and all its obligations and the Vietnam anxiety. Let's start unloading the truck."

As they walked outside, they heard the grinding roar of a large construction vehicle coming up the street. Rory raced past them and ran to the front gate just in time to see a bright yellow Caterpillar front loader parking in front of the Ryder truck. A tall dark haired man, dressed in black, with a priest's collar and strangely out of place, heavy work boots, climbed down from the cab. "What in the world?" Livy whispered.

Branch shook his head. "I have no idea," he answered, as the man approached them and held out his hand.

"Hello, you moving in today?" the priest asked, shaking Branch's hand and smiling at Livy and Rory. "I'm Father Michael. I live in the house up on the hill," he said in a thick Boston accent.

Branch smiled and shook the priest's hand. "Happy to meet you. I'm Branch Monroe and this is my wife Livy and our daughter Rory. And yes, we're moving in."

"Well, welcome to the neighborhood. I've been here a couple of years. It's a good street and you've got one of the nicest houses. Let me know if I can be of any help," he offered, waving good-bye and climbing back into the front loader.

Branch unlocked the truck cargo door while Livy and Rory watched as the big machine drove up the mansion's driveway and parked. "Did you know there was a rectory or manse on the street?"

Livy asked in a low voice. "I mean where's the church and why is he driving a construction vehicle? Don't you think it's strange?"

Branch shrugged. "He seems nice enough, but it does seem weird. We'll ask the Bakers about him."

()

Chapter 5

Late in the day, Georgia and Ed Baker welcomed their new tenants with a basket of fruit and cookies. "We're so glad you're here," Georgia gushed. "We didn't know what to expect when we put the house up for rent and then thank God, you took it right away. We feel blessed."

"It's our first time being landlords," Ed added. "You said you sold your house in Virginia before moving here. So you already know how to take care of a house. That's a great comfort for us."

Branch laughed. "That's right. It was a much newer home, but we did a lot of work on it. Of course, some maintenance doesn't change no matter how old a house is."

"I grew up in an old house and you just get used to appreciating the old features and all the quirks," Livy added. "This one is beautiful and you've done such a great job with the upkeep. Has it always been in your family?"

Georgia shook her head. "Oh no. We just bought it from Martha Sutter a few months ago. She owns the old mansion up on the hill. Years ago, her house and your house were the only homes here. Sutter Court was the drive up to the main house and all the land surrounding it as far as you could see and beyond was their property. Martha's father built your house as a marriage cottage for her and her fiancee.

Sadly, the wedding never took place, but the house was always Martha's. She lived in it for years, even after she became deaf and unable to speak. Her niece Hope grew up with parents who were also deaf mutes, so she knew sign language. After Hope's parents died, she moved into the cottage with Martha to help her. When Martha's father died, she decided to move into the big house by herself. Hope stayed in this cottage for a while, but when Martha became wheelchair bound and needed full time help, Hope moved in with her and this sweet little house sat empty."

"When Martha decided to sell it, we bought it right away to keep that Father Michael from getting it. We don't trust him one bit," Ed chimed in. "He claims he married Hope at some point after he moved into the big house, but we don't believe him. Now he's trying to buy up other houses on the street. He even made us an offer, but we would never sell or rent to him."

"Is he the guy, in the priest collar, driving the front loader?" Livy asked. "We met him earlier. He kind of looks like Rock Hudson."

Georgia nodded. "That's him, but he's not really a priest. He says he went to Yale, but we don't believe that one either. He's some sort of spiritualist and he's formed a commune here called Ways. He calls it a sacred experiment in communal living. He's attracting all sorts of people to the Sutter property. Some are living up there and others just gather there. They call themselves Ways. Apparently, Martha and Hope have joined up too. At least that's what we're hearing."

"So that's why he needs other properties on the street, especially those closest to the mansion. He wants to house more

Ways members," Branch mused. "I guess you had to buy this house as a buffer to protect yourselves from the commune."

Ed stood up to leave and motioned to Georgia. "That was pretty much our idea. But you folks don't need to worry. Ways seems like a harmless group so far, and you aren't the type of insecure, needy people Father Michael is mostly looking for. You're here to get a professional degree and move on. You don't need the support he's offering through the commune. If you need anything or have questions about the house, call us anytime."

"It's getting to be dinner time. Did you stop for groceries on your way in?" Georgia asked.

"Yes, we're fine," Livy smiled. She closed the front door, turned on the porch light and glared at Branch. "You should have asked more questions about this neighborhood. Would you have rented this house if you'd known we'd be living next to a commune?"

"Well I didn't know, ok," Branch snapped, raising his voice. "The street looked normal to me and the house is great. The Bakers seem like nice old fashioned people, even though they dress alike and look like camp counselors and use the same black dye on their hair. Don't you see? They didn't mention the commune because they wanted us to rent the house because we're not like Father Michael and his Ways people. And now we're here and we have to make the best of it."

Rory had stopped playing with her toys and was staring at her parents. The sound of their raised voices made her start to cry and Livy picked her up. "Let's not fight about this. Hopefully, Ed Baker is right and Ways will leave us alone. I'll find something for dinner," she mumbled.

()

chapter 6

A few days later, Hope and Father Michael walked hand-in-hand down Sutter Court to Branch and Livy's house and rang the bell. Rory rushed to the door, looked through the glass and waved, while Livy unlocked the door and opened it slightly. Michael smiled. "Hi Livy, I wanted to introduce you to my wife Hope.

"I've been looking forward to meeting you," Hope said quietly and handed Livy a white flowering plant."

Livy opened the door wider. "Thank you. It's beautiful. We're still getting settled, but please come in. What kind of plant is this?"

Hope smiled. "It's called a Peace Lily because the flowers look like white flags of peace. My aunt loves them and grows lots of them in her plant room."

Livy motioned to the living room and set the plant on the coffee table. "Would you like to sit down? I'll have to leave soon to pick up Branch at the University, but we could visit for a minute. He's buying all his books today."

"That's right. Classes start tomorrow," Michael said, sitting down with Hope on one of the soft, comfortable couches. "We have some students living with us, and they're getting ready too.

You and Branch and Rory ought to come up and meet them. In fact, we're having services at sundown tonight. You should come."

Livy was still standing near the pocket doors, but she nervously backed up a few steps. "Oh no! We can't. We're still too busy sorting out things here. But thank you for stopping by and for the beautiful lily. I'd like to see your aunt's plant room sometime. Sorry, but Rory and I are going to have to leave now," she said in a rush, opening the front door.

Outside, Father Michael chided Hope. "That didn't go very well did it. Why didn't you back me up about them coming up for services? We need more well educated, upwardly mobile people to join Ways. I'm guessing they have family money too."

Hope reached for his hand. "I like her, Michael. Besides you and Aunt Martha, I don't have any real friends. Maybe Livy and I could be friends. I'll work on her, but let's not pressure them to come to Ways. Let it happen naturally, like you and I found each other without trying."

Father Michael put his arm around her shoulders. Of course, Hope had never suspected his attraction to her was solely based on acquiring the Sutter property. She was lonely and clueless. It was easy to manipulate her and convince her to marry him. "All right, we'll try it your way for a while. You get to know Livy and I will do the same with Branch. But remember our goal as always is to bring them into our fold, transfer their money to us, and make them become completely dependent on Ways."

Hope started to shiver and Father Michael pulled her closer. "What's wrong? Why are you shaking?"

"It's nothing, just a little fall chill in the air. Look, the leaves are all starting to turn," she murmured and pointed to the trees. But silently she was thinking about Livy, Branch and Rory and their happy, normal life. It was the type of life she had never known, growing up in a silent house with her deaf, mute parents who died young, and then living with her eccentric aunt with the same silent afflictions. She was grateful to Michael and Ways for rescuing her from the lonely spinster life of caring for her aging aunt. But he was very demanding about her participating in the communal life, the sharing of all food and clothing, the living and sleeping together, the constant household chores and childcare.

Sometimes she wondered about Michael's true feelings for her. Although he had performed their wedding ceremony and treated her as his wife, she felt panicked when he forced himself on her, but then angry and jealous when he slept with other women in the group. So far she had been able to hold off advances from other men in the commune, but Michael continually lectured her about the sin of not being giving of herself. It seemed she had gone from living one abnormal life to being trapped in another.

Aunt Martha, on the other hand, not only accepted Michael, but seemed to love him. She knew little about the commune arrangement and didn't question him about it. He was especially kind and respectful to her. She held tightly to his hand and smiled while he sat close to her and described (while Hope signed) the improvements he was making to the house and property. Under his supervision, his workers had updated the electrical systems and the plumbing in the mansion, the barn, and the outbuildings. Outdoors, they had patched the roof shingles, replaced the gutters and down-spouts, painted the exterior of the house, kept the lawn mowed and fertilized and the trees and bushes pruned. At the end of each of these intimate sessions, Michael would kiss her hand and Aunt Martha would sign the same thing, "I always knew you would come back to me."

And Hope always wondered the same thing. "Who did Aunt Martha think Michael was?"

()

Chapter 7

The fall passed quickly for the Monroes. Branch's classes were demanding and time consuming. Livy found a good daycare for Rory at the University's preschool educational training program, and soon after that, she lucked into a job at the town's Hall of Records.

From time to time, they saw Father Michael on the street usually at the end of the day. He and Branch talked about the Northeast or sports or sometimes the construction job he was on. Each time he would end the conversation by inviting them to evening services and they always turned him down. It became so repetitive that they all began laughing about it. Finally one day, Father Michael said, "One of these days your curiosity about us and our way of life will become irresistible and you will join us."

Branch frowned and pursed his lips. "I enjoy our conversations Father Michael and we appreciate your invitations, but Ways is not for us. It would be better if you stopped asking us."

Father Michael laughed and waved good-bye. "Wait and see Branch. You will eventually come."

Livy waved and pulled Branch away. "You have to stop talking to him so much. Stop letting him think you're his friend."

"I'm okay being casual friends with him, as long as he

doesn't get too close. But what about you and Hope? I see you two sitting on the porch talking and her bringing little toys for Rory. Don't you think it's ironic she brought you a Peace Lily as a house-warming gift?" he asked.

Livy sighed. "I feel sorry for her. She seems so lonely and confused. I don't think she's ever talked much to another woman outside of her family. And that must have been strange too with all the conversations in sign language."

Branch shrugged. "She seems happy with Michael. How could she be lonely living in a commune? I mean everything is share this and share that."

"That's just it. I don't think Hope is happy sharing Father Michael with the others, especially the women. She says he's upset with her for not having sex with the other men.," Livy answered. "She told you that?" Branch said in a low voice.

Livy shook her head again. "Not exactly, but she talked around it. She mentioned that five or six of the other women are pregnant. She said any of the men up there could be the fathers including Father Michael. And you know, I think Hope is pregnant too. She's not showing yet, but she's asked me questions about what it's like to have a baby and she pays close attention to everything Rory does."

Branch took Livy's hand. "I know you like to help people, but try not to get too involved with Hope. You don't want her to pull you into that situation up there at the mansion. We still don't really know for sure what, if anything strange, is going on there."

Livy took a deep breath. "What's going on up there is not right. It sounds evil to me or at the very least illegal. Maybe they don't know it yet, but Hope and her aunt are caught in the middle of it."

()

Chapter 8

The Saturday after Thanksgiving was a brisk, sunny day. That afternoon, Branch and Livy set out with Rory on a treasure hunt walk around the neighborhood. She carried a little pink bucket for collecting feathers, rocks, pinecones and other special finds. As usual Rory excitedly ran ahead of her parents even as they called to her to come back. They liked to explore surrounding streets but, on this particular day their walk took them up Sutter Court to the base of the driveway to the mansion. Branch and Livy stopped, but Rory kept running up toward the house.

"Stop! Rory! Stop!" Branch and Livy both called out as they ran after her, but Rory kept going past the side of the house and out of view.

"Where is she going?" Livy cried out breathlessly trying to keep up with Branch. He didn't answer, but instead ran faster leaving Livy behind.

The front loader was parked over to the side next to an old worn path that led around the house and sloped downward as far as he could see. It looked like it might have been a wagon trail to the outer fields at one time. Dense woods were on one side and stones were rising up through tall grass on the other. Branch could see Rory's white Irish knit hat with a pompom bobbing up in the grass. "I see her!" he shouted back to Livy. But then he lost sight of her again. "Rory ! Rory!" he shouted just as Livy caught up with him. "She's over there somewhere," he panted and pointed into the thick waist high, weeds.

Livy started hysterically screaming over and over, "Rory where are you?" but the little girl didn't answer. Instead two tall dark figures appeared up close to the back of the house on the distant side of the tall grass.

"Who's there?" one of them shouted.

Recognizing the Boston accent, Branch yelled, "Father Michael is that you? It's Branch and Livy. Rory is lost somewhere in all these tall weeds. Can you help us find her?"

"We'll walk in from this side!" Father Michael shouted back, motioning to the other men and women who had appeared at his side. Calling Rory's name over and over, Branch and Livy and the others waded through the weeds from both sides. The uneven ground was treacherous and everyone tripped over large stones and sometimes suddenly fell into large rectangular holes.

At last a woman called out, "Livy it's Hope. We've got her. She's here by the big stone in the middle of the field."

Branch and Livy and the other searchers pushed their way to the big stone structure rising above the weeds. Rory was calmly sitting in front of a metal door in the stone and staring up at all the people around her. The name Sutter was carved into the stone above the door. Her little pink bucket was by her side. "Look Mama, look what I found," she said. In one hand she held a large ornate key and in the other were bleached white bone fragments that vaguely resembled a hand.

Horrified, Livy kneeled down beside her. "Oh Rory, are you all right? she asked, looking at her scratched face and hands. A bloody cut knee was showing through her torn overalls.

"Hurts," she said, touching her knee. Only when Livy took the key and bones from Rory and laid them on the ground did the little girl start to cry. "Mine, mine," she kept saying even after Branch picked her up.

"It'll be okay," he said quietly, trying to soothe her. "Let's go home and fix your knee. Thank you everyone for your help," he said to the crowd and turned around to find the quickest way out of the weeds.

Father Michael took hold of Livy's arm and motioned to Branch. "I'll lead you out. Walk this way up closer to the house. It'll be easier," he said, leading them through the choking weeds.

Livy glanced up at the back of the house and for a moment saw an old woman's face, framed in white hair and what looked like leaves, staring down at them through the glass walls. But the uneven rocky ground and weeds forced her to look down to keep from falling. When she was able to look up again, the face in the leaves had disappeared.

After they reached the driveway, Branch thanked Father Michael. "We can make it from here. We can't thank you enough for your help. We never meant to intrude on the property. Rory just took off. It won't happen again."

Father Michael smiled. "I've told you. You're welcome here anytime. It's just probably not best to start your visit at the back of the house," he chuckled.

"Was that an old family cemetery back there?" Livy asked.

Father Michael nodded. "We've made excellent progress updating the house and the barn. Both buildings are great for large groups to congregate for meals and evening services. And we've finished converting the other outbuildings into living quarters. Cleaning up the cemetery is not our responsibility. Maybe we'll get to it eventually, but so far Miss Sutter doesn't want us to touch it. It's a shame the cemetery is where you started your first visit here."

By now they were at the bottom of the driveway. Livy shivered. "Thank you again for your help," she said touching Father Michael's arm.

He waved and stood watching them walk away. "Shit, what a disaster. Not a good way to impress them to join us," he said under his breath.

"That place is a horror show!" Branch exploded as soon as they got home. "I can't believe the town, if they know about it, is letting the cemetery exist in that condition with all the old caved in graves and bones lying around. You're right. I was wrong to rent this house."

"Calm down Branch," Livy tried to soothe him. "That was a horrible experience, but thank God, Rory is all right. Let's clean her up in a warm bath and bandage that knee. We need to be calm for her. We can talk about all of this later after she goes to bed."

Branch agreed, but Rory complained through the bath and kept crying and saying, "Mine, Mine!" She was too upset about her lost treasures to eat dinner and only fell fitfully asleep in bed with Livy cuddling her. Afterwards, Branch poured two glasses of wine and they sat quietly together trying to understand the whole nightmarish experience.

"What on earth is going on up there Branch?" Livy sighed. "I mean none of those people, especially Father Michael and Hope, seemed surprised that Rory was sitting there with human bones in her hand. Poor baby. I still can't believe it happened."

"I'm wondering who's been disturbing those graves and why? How long has that been going on? Some or all of those holes we fell in were probably old graves. I'm surprised Rory was able to climb out of them. Martha Sutter and Hope have been living up there for years. They must know about the condition of the cemetery. Why wouldn't they do something about it?" Branch fumed.

Livy stood up. "I'm going to check on Rory and then try to get some sleep. But I've decided that now I've learned my way around the Hall of Records, I'm going to do some research on the Sutter family and that property. Maybe I'll find some answers."

"That's a good idea," Branch agreed. "You know the Christmas break starts in a couple of weeks. Maybe we could get out of here and go to your parents' house in Nashville for a few days. What do you think?"

"I would love that," Livy smiled and kissed him. "Getting away will be good for all of us!

()

Chapter 9

Hope had been helping her Aunt Martha get settled in bed even before her arthritis and balance issues began preventing her from climbing stairs. Although she could still walk short distances while holding on to furniture or walls, she rarely left her wheelchair without Hope's help. Using a standard toilet had become impossible for the two of them to manage. So Hope had found an adult potty chair with a chamber pot that slid underneath and had installed it in the small bathroom off the library. This allowed Martha to stand and move from the wheelchair to the potty chair by herself and maintain some privacy. For Hope who managed the cleanup, it was a messy solution at best. And even though Martha could manage the walk-in shower fitted with a seat, she still preferred to rely on Hope to provide daily sponge baths which she sarcastically referred to as bird baths.

Their late afternoon routine included an early dinner around five o'clock in the solarium, followed by a glass of sherry for Martha. Afterwards Martha wheeled herself into the library where Hope had already prepared her bed with daily fresh linens. Hope helped her undress, use the potty chair, change into a silk nightgown, and settle into bed. Usually Martha let Hope stow her jewelry in a lock box kept in a secret compartment behind a built in corner cupboard. It swung open when a small lever was pressed under a shelf. But sometimes she preferred to sleep in her jewels and dream in her elegance. Martha liked to fall asleep reading, so Hope would check on her before she went to her room upstairs and turned down the lights. If Martha needed her during the night, she rang a loud bell which echoed through the silent house and woke Hope.

One evening after Rory was lost in the cemetery, Martha motioned to Hope to sit with her for a while after she settled into bed. She began the signing conversation with, "I've been thinking about those people in our cemetery? Who were they?"

"They're the ones who rented your old cottage from the Bakers in September. Their names are Branch and Livy Monroe," Hope answered.

Martha stopped her with her hand. "And the little girl?"

Hope sighed. "That's Rory. She's adorable. I want one just like her."

Martha frowned. "That's our cemetery. We're the only ones who should be in there."

"I know Aunt Martha. It was an accident. Rory ran into the tall grass and got lost. We helped her parents find her. It was a terrible experience for them. I don't think they'll be coming back. Michael is very upset about that. He is obsessed about convincing them to join us in Ways."

The mention of Michael made Martha smile and she seemed to forget the cemetery incident. "Where is he? I need him to sit with me while I fall asleep. He brings me peace just like he did years ago when we were young."

"He's a very comforting man," Hope agreed. "But he can't come to you now. He's busy preparing for the evening services and he's probably wondering where I am. I'm supposed to attend too."

Disappointed, Martha closed her eyes and dismissed Hope with a wave. Hope kissed her on the cheek and quietly left the room. After she was gone, Martha opened her eyes and saw herself as a young woman in her late twenties. It was years before the onset of the hereditary Meniere's Disease left her deaf and speechless, and before Michael went off to fight in World War II in Europe. They were alone in the newly built marriage cottage before it was furnished, and they were dancing and laughing through the empty rooms. Happiness and the future had no bounds for them, but later on that turned into a cruel joke for her.

After he left for Europe, she had moved into the cottage as planned and stayed there, waiting for him to come back to her. When his letters stopped coming she thought he must have been killed or severely injured. Later she found out that wasn't the case at all. He had fallen in love with a woman in Paris, married her and never came back. Why had he come now? And why was he still young and handsome while she was so miserably deaf, old and crippled? Tears trickled through the wrinkles in her cheeks and neck until sleep finally came to her rescue.

Meanwhile, Hope decided not to help Michael with the Ways evening services. Instead she went upstairs and took a long hot bath. It felt delicious to get away by herself behind the locked bathroom door. She ran her hands over her growing abdomen, closed her eyes and feeling the tiniest of movements, thought of the life inside her. She hadn't told anyone, not even Michael about the baby. She hadn't even seen a doctor because of course, Michael wouldn't want her to do that. There were other pregnant Ways women, and she was certain they weren't seeing doctors either. One of the rules was that Ways would take care of themselves in sickness and in all other things, without help from outsiders.

She was going to have to tell Michael soon though because her clothes weren't fitting and her thin body was becoming more and more pear shaped. And then there was Aunt Martha. How would she react to this news? As far as Hope could tell, Martha had no idea that she and Michael were married. The older woman was lost in the idea that Michael was her long lost fiancee who had returned to her at last. Michael continued to let her believe that lie, as he sat beside her holding her hand while they wrote notes back and forth to each other on chalkboards. In fact, after moving in, Michael had begun the note writing with Martha and told Hope her presence wasn't constantly needed for the sign language. Now she had no idea what Michael might be telling her aunt or trying to convince her to do.

"Are you in there Hope?" Father Michael called and knocked on the door.

Hope quickly wrapped up in a towel. "I'm just getting out of a bath. I'll be out in a minute."

Father Michael, still dressed in his priest clothes, was propped up on the bed when Hope walked in. "Why did you have the door locked?" he asked.

"I just wanted a little privacy and a nice bath. I never know who's roaming around up here," she explained.

Father Michael patted the bed for her to sit next to him. "So I guess you weren't trying to keep me out."

Hope stretched out next to him. "Of course not. Did you look in on Aunt Martha before you came upstairs?"

"I did, but she seemed to be sleeping, so I didn't stay. Tell me more about this disease that caused her deafness. When did she get it?" he asked.

Hope sighed. "It's called Meniere's Disease and it's a very sad story. Are you sure you want to hear it?"

Father Michael took her hand. "Please tell me. It will help me to better understand you and your family," he said softly.

"The sudden onset of deafness in adults has been around probably since the beginning of mankind. Sometimes it's caused by a severe illness or a loud explosion," Hope explained. "Aunt Martha's and my father's deafness was caused by a fluid buildup in the inner ear. That results in severe vertigo, loud ear ringing and intense ear pressure. Sometimes it only affects one ear at first, but usually both ears develop it. Some people lose their minds because they can't cope with the unbearably severe symptoms."

"And there's no cure?" Father Michael asked.

Hope shook her head. "No, not so far. Sometime in the late 1800's a French doctor named Meniere identified the disorder as an inner ear problem. It was named Meniere's Disease after his findings. Up until then, doctors had diagnosed it as a brain disease and patients were sent to asylums for the rest of their lives."

Father Michael frowned. "Are you worried you might get it too?"

"It's possible Michael because it is considered a genetic risk.

The symptoms usually start sometime after age forty, but Aunt Martha started having progressive symptoms in her twenties. My father must have been in his late thirties or maybe forty when he got it."

"What about your mother? Wasn't she deaf too?" Father Michael asked.

Hope shook her head. " No. She didn't have Meniere's. She was born deaf. She was teaching a sign language course when she met my father."

"What about your grandfather?" Father Michael persisted.

"He didn't have it," Hope answered quickly. "Aunt Martha thinks her mother, my grandmother, must have had the gene which she passed on to her children. But she remembers her as a lively beautiful woman, talking and singing and enjoying life. Sadly, she died when my father was born. So no one knows if she would have eventually had Meniere's disease."

Hope sighed. "It's still considered sort of a mystery disease. Aunt Martha will never get better. So yes, I worry that one day the symptoms will start, but there's nothing I can do to prevent it."

Father Michael put his arm around her and pulled her close. "You're right. This is a very sad family tragedy, but I think you are very brave. Let's add to our prayer list the finding of a miracle cure for Martha and a protective spiritual shield around you, so you won't get the disease. And from now on, we should take precautions before we have sex. We don't want to risk passing this on to another generation."

Hope giggled and pulled his hand across her abdomen. "It's a little late for precautions."

Father Michael angrily jerked his hand away. "You're already pregnant! When exactly were you going to tell me?" he seethed.

Hope's eyes filled with tears and she got up and moved across the room away from him. "I was waiting to be sure. I thought you'd be happy, but now I can see you never wanted this."

Father Michael got up and went to the door. "It's a big surprise. I hadn't planned on taking on the responsibility of a child with you yet. And especially not now, knowing that not only you, but this baby may have this terrible disease. We have so much work to do for Ways. I consider everyone here as one of my children. Our mission—yours and mine—is to take care of them and bring others into our community. We don't have time for disabled children of our own."

Hope's soft voice turned hard and shrill. "Do you even listen to what you're preaching to others? Every night you go on and on about the value of communal living and the sharing of everything including our bodies. What did you think was going to happen with us? Half of the women here are pregnant. Maybe some of them are having your babies too. What about them? Do you have time for them? At least I'm certain this baby is yours because I have refused advances from other men here, even though you criticize me for it."

Father Michael lunged across the room and slapped her. Surprised, she sank down on the rug and covered her face. "This is Ways' house Hope, and I forbid you to talk to me like that ever again. Any children living here are children of Ways. This child will be raised like the others. It won't be yours. Understand?"

Hope nodded silently and watched as Father Michael

stormed out of the room. After a few minutes, she gathered herself up off the floor and opened her vanity drawer where she kept a collection of keys. She pulled out a slim door key and locked the bedroom door. Then she leaned against it and whispered, "You're wrong Michael. This baby will always be mine and the Sutter house will always belong to Aunt Martha and me. I will do all I have to do to keep you and Ways from ever having it. "

()

Chapter 10

December was a slow month in the Oakton Hall Of Records office. People were concentrating on holiday shopping and preparations. Most property transfers and other transactions were postponed until the new year. The office would be closed for the week between Christmas and New Year's Day. For Livy, the light workload offered time to research the Sutter property.

She began by looking through the old land maps from the early 1800's. There she found the Sutter name on all the land east of the village of Oakton. As the years passed, recorded land sales showed the Sutter family had gradually enriched themselves by selling off large tracts of land, first for small farms and later for commercial development. The last entries were for multi-family neighborhoods.

Martha Sutter's father Abel kept all the land surrounding the mansion for the family's private estate. And just as the Bakers had said, Branch and Livy's marriage cottage was the only other house on the estate. Toward the end of his life in the early 1950's, Abel divided the land lining the long driveway into half acre lots and sold them to builders. That's when the Sutter driveway became the residential street Sutter Court.

Martha's brother Andrew and his wife Edna built a house

on one of those lots and lived there until they died. Livy guessed they were Hope's parents because she was eventually listed as selling the property. That was probably when she moved into the cottage with Martha.

The history of the family cemetery was sketchy. It did not appear on the land maps until Abel had the mausoleum built in 1955. Earlier family members were most likely buried in those very old in-ground graves she and Branch had tripped over that frightening day.

Livy's next stop was the town library where she researched old newspapers from 1955. An article with a picture of the Sutter mausoleum noted it was the first above ground burial structure in the area. A few months later, Abel's obituary appeared and place of burial was listed as the Sutter Family Cemetery. After that the town listed it as a private cemetery on a residential street.

"So nobody really knows how many people may have been buried back there since the 1800's," Branch said when Livy told him about her research.

"And it doesn't help explain the disturbed graves we stumbled into or the bone fragments lying around," Livy added.

"Father Michael says he's going to clean it up," Branch reminded her. "But what if it's the commune members disturbing the graves for some kind of cult ceremony?"

"I'm so glad we're going home next week," Livy shivered. "I can't get past what happened to Rory and I don't want to even think about what else might be happening up there."

Branch shook his head. "I shouldn't have said that about a cult ceremony. We don't know for sure that anything bad at all is happening there. What if Father Michael's Ways really is just a harmless group of people enjoying communal living? At least let's hope that's the case."

Livy smiled. "I love it that you're trying to be so optimistic, while I'm so suspicious. I hope you're right, but I just can't help having such a bad feeling."

()

Chapter 11

The Christmas break at Livy's parents' home in Nashville felt like a tonic. Rory, as the only grandchild was the center of attention, and of course could do no wrong. Livy's Mom and Dad provided a relaxed visit with lots of food and holiday gifts. Afterwards, Branch and Livy were rested and happy on the trip home to Oakton. Gone were the gnawing thoughts that something bad could be happening there.

Late afternoon snow was falling when they pulled up in front of the cottage on Sutter Court. Rory jumped out of the car and tried to catch snowflakes on her tongue. Branch carried the suitcases to the front porch while Livy gathered up the pile of new toys and gifts. When she approached the porch, Branch yelled

"Stay back. Don't come up here. Take Rory back to the car!"

"What's wrong?" Livy cried.

"Just get in the car. I'll be out there in a minute," he yelled again, as he disappeared into the house.

Livy grabbed Rory and pushed her back into the car with all the presents and then locked all the doors.

Rory started to cry. "Where Daddy go, Mama?"

"It's all right sweetheart. Daddy's just checking something

in the house. He'll be out in a minute," Livy answered, but her voice sounded weak and her hands were trembling.

A few minutes later, Branch came out carrying a towel and covered something on the front porch by the door. He took a deep breath and motioned to Livy to get out of the car. "There's a pile of dead animals surrounded by candles on the porch. I've covered them up so Rory won't see them. The front door was open and the television was on in the living room. Looks like someone has been sleeping in our bed, and there are dirty dishes piled in the kitchen sink. The back door in the basement is open, and there are footprints in the snow."

Rory pounded her little fists on the car window and screamed, "Mama, Out! Out! Out!"

"You're sure there's no one in there now?" Livy asked.

Branch shook his head. "No, they're gone. I'll get Rory and lock the car. We might as well go in and get out of the cold. We'll have to tell the Bakers and call the police right away."

Livy was surprised by the large towel covered pile by the door, but she kept quiet, hoping that Rory wouldn't notice as Branch carried her into the house. Thankfully, the house felt warm and cozy. The couches and pillows in the living room were rumpled and the television was on, but the rest of the room was just as they had left it. Rory's room was undisturbed and she ran in, pulled off her coat and hat and started playing with her toys. Branch put his arm around Livy. "Don't start cleaning up until the police come," he said, picking up the phone. He called Ed Baker who immediately called the police and then quickly came over.

Ed was wearing slippers and still had a dinner napkin

tucked under his chin when he arrived. He lifted the towel and looked at the pile of dead animals and the weird circle of candles around them. "Damnation! Who does stuff like this?" he sputtered as he walked through the house. "Nothing like this has ever happened on Sutter Court, and we've been here thirty years. How'd they get in?"

"I'm not sure. The front door was open, so they could have come in that way, but they definitely ran out through the back basement door. That door was wide open and there were tracks in the snow out back," Branch said, pointing out the sunroom window into the back yard.

Ed shook his head. "You've been gone for a week. We can see your backyard from our house. You'd think we would have noticed if something was going on over here."

Livy walked into the sunroom. "Maybe they came and went in the dark. I mean they could have come in through the back, unlocked the front door, and then used either door to come and go. When they heard us coming home, they ran away."

"Damnation!" Ed repeated when the doorbell started ringing.

Two uniformed policemen stood outside the front door when Branch answered. "I'm Officer John Williams and this is my partner Officer Fred Holmes. We got a call that you folks have had a burglary. Is this part of it?" he asked, pointing to the towel.

"Thanks for coming. I'm Branch Monroe. There's a pile of dead animals and candles under there. We don't know what that means. I covered it so our daughter wouldn't see it. The front door was ajar when we got here."

Ed Baker was standing behind Branch. "I called you. My wife and I live next door. We own this house too. Branch and his wife and daughter are our tenants."

"Come in," Branch said. "We waited for you to get here before we started cleaning up. We've been away for a week."

The officers looked through the house and basement and took notes and pictures. The basement back door was still open, but the footprints in the back yard had disappeared under the falling snow. "Anything missing?" Officer Williams asked.

"We don't know yet," Branch answered. After we clean up, we'll have a better idea."

"You'll have to wait on that until we've dusted for fingerprints," Officer Holmes said. "We have a fingerprint kit in the car. I'll bring it in and take your prints now and yours too, Mr. Baker. Would you mind asking your wife to come over so we can take hers too? That way we can eliminate all of you and concentrate on identifying any others we find."

"Certainly, I'll go get her now," Ed said, hurrying out the door.

"How long will this fingerprinting take?" Livy asked. "And what about our little girl? She's only two years old."

Officer Williams smiled. "The process doesn't take long and we don't fingerprint two year-olds, but if she wants us to, we will." And of course, when Rory watched Officer Holmes fingerprinting Branch and Livy, she stuck her fingers out too and laughed as he printed her tiny finger tips.

Ed and Georgia were next and then both police officers dusted for prints on the front and back doors and the hard surfaces in the dining room which Branch and Livy were using as their bedroom. They also took prints off the kitchen appliances, counter tops and the wooden table and chairs. "I think that should do it," Officer Holmes finally said. "You can begin cleaning up now. Let us know right away if anything has been stolen. "

"Just one last thing, besides the Bakers, who knew you were going away?" Officer Williams asked.

Branch ran his fingers through his hair. "I told a few of my friends from school, but they all went away for the Christmas break. They're probably not back yet."

Officer Holmes turned to Livy. "What about you Mrs. Monroe? Did you tell anyone?"

"My supervisor Mrs. Grimes at my office knew, because I asked to take a couple of extra days off beyond the week it was closed for the holidays. Rory's daycare at the University closed before we left, so I didn't tell them. That's about it," Livy answered.

"Mr. and Mrs. Baker, did you happen to tell anyone the Monroes were away?" Officer Holmes asked.

Ed shrugged. "We may have mentioned it to our daughter Lou Ann and her husband. They were with us for Christmas dinner. I can't think of anyone else," he said and looked at Georgia who shook her head.

The officers closed their notebooks. "You need to call one of us if something is missing or you think of anything you've forgotten to tell us," Officer Williams instructed.

Both men handed Branch their cards. "We'll send animal control over tomorrow to pick up the dead animals. The candle holders look to be antique silver. We'll take them with us. Maybe they will tell us something about who left them here."

Livy drew in her breath. "I just remembered I told Hope Sutter Brown we were going away. She lives in the mansion up on the hill."

Officer Williams opened his notebook again. "Why did you tell her? Are you friends?"

"We've gotten to know each other over the last few months. She stopped by here a couple days before we left to invite us to Christmas dinner at their house. I told her we couldn't come because we were going to see my parents for the week."

"That's it." Officer Williams said.

Livy nodded. "Pretty much. She wished us a Merry Christmas and said we were lucky to have parents to be with during the holidays. Then she added something about how we'd be missing a very special evening at their house."

"There's your answer!" Ed interrupted. "There's a fellow named Michael Brown who lives in the Sutter house. He dresses like a priest and calls himself a spiritualist. Personally, I think he's got some kind of cult going on up there. He calls it Ways. Now there's all sorts of undesirable strangers going up there especially in the evening."

"Is this Michael Brown related to Hope Sutter Brown?" Officer Holmes asked.

"She's his wife." Livy answered.

Ed raised his eyebrows. "Really! Do you actually believe they're married? Wonder what Martha Sutter thinks of that or if she even knows. I thought maybe Hope just took his name as part of the cult thing."

"And Martha Sutter is?" Officer Williams asked.

"She owns the Sutter property. Hope is her niece," Ed explained.

Livy frowned. "Honestly, Officer, Hope is such a sweet girl. I can't imagine her ever having anything to do with what happened here."

Officer Williams looked at Officer Holmes who nodded. "Okay then. I think you folks can start cleaning up and trying to get settled for the night. You should change the locks on both the doors right away. It appears they maybe had a key, or someone else let them in. There's no sign of an unlocked or broken door or window, but even if nothing has been stolen, we would still consider this a burglary or criminal trespass that needs investigation," he said. Both officers shook everyone's hands and left, saying they'd be in touch.

Branch closed the door, but he and Ed watched through the glass as the officers dusted the candlesticks for fingerprints and then bagged them. When they drove away, they went to the top of the street and parked in front of the Sutter driveway.

Ed and Georgia turned to leave. "I'll have a locksmith over here first thing tomorrow. Hopefully, he can just add dead bolt locks and preserve the antique lock on the front door. It's a beauty," he said, as they shuffled off through the snow.

Branch put his arms around Livy. "It's going to be all right, honey. I'll get the rest of our stuff out of the car, just in case someone gets another idea about helping themselves to our things. And then I'll move some furniture in front of the doors for the night. That way we'll be able to hear if someone tries to get in again."

Livy's hands were shaking. "This is all so creepy. Someone's been in here going through our things, sleeping in our bed and who knows what else. I've never thought about owning a gun, but I wish we had one now. I know you learned how to shoot in the Navy. I feel so angry and afraid, but at the same time guilty that I brought Hope up to the police. I don't want them to bother her."

()

Chapter 12

After his fight with Hope, Father Michael left the house and walked the neighborhood, trying to work through his situation with Hope and the news about the baby. He knew he shouldn't have hit her, but he was just so angry about the baby and her disobedience. There was no room for that behavior in Ways and certainly not from his own wife. Worse, he thought she was an idiot for possibly passing along a genetic disease. He had married her to ensure he could obtain Martha's property, not to possibly perpetuate a hereditary ailment. It was snowing lightly when he returned to the mansion and went to his office in a second floor alcove at the top of the winding staircase. He sat down at his desk facing the windows and stared down the front lawn and Sutter Court below. The rolling lawn and the tree lined street glistened in the freshly fallen snow. Even though it had been dark for hours, the snow cast a bright light on the peaceful scene. As he sat staring, he noticed car lights pulling away from the front of Branch and Livy's cottage.

The car slowly drove up the street and parked across the base of the mansion driveway. "What's he doing?" he whispered and fumbled around in the desk drawer for binoculars. He stood close to the windows and adjusted the lenses. Only then did he realize he was looking at a police car with two policemen inside. He lowered the binoculars and slowly backed away. He wondered if they were looking at him at the same time.

Father Michael sat back down and watched the car until it pulled away after about twenty minutes. Then he hurried down the hall to tell Hope what he had just seen, but the door was locked. He knocked and softly called her name, but she didn't answer. He walked on down the hallway and opened the door to one of the other bedrooms. No one was sleeping in there at the moment and the bed linens appeared to be fresh. He closed the door and lay down, but his brain would not let him sleep. All night he kept seeing the police car. What did they want? Were they under suspicion for something? Would his Ways plans be interrupted? And Hope—what was he going to do about her? She was supposed to be his insurance policy for gaining the property. And what about Martha? He wished she would just give up and die, but that didn't seem to be happening. He should start planning her death soon. All these thoughts kept swirling through his mind until finally he got up at early dawn and went down to the kitchen.

He smiled and switched on one of the coffee machines. Hope was very good at managing the kitchen for Ways. She made certain food and drinks were readily available for the adults and children. No one ever went hungry. Each night she always set up the kitchen for the next morning's breakfast. Two large coffeemakers were ready to go. Bowls for cereal and instant oatmeal were set out, as well as bread for toast, along with big bowls of bananas and apples. Large pitchers of milk and orange juice sat ready in the refrigerator.

Father Michael poured himself a cup of coffee and went into the sitting room. Through the glass French doors he could see a light shining in the library. He cracked open the doors and stepped through to see if Martha was awake. Wrapped in her lace shawl, she was sitting up in bed reading one of her botanical books. She jumped and then smiled when he appeared beside her. "Sorry, I didn't mean to scare you," he mouthed to her and patted his heart.

Martha pointed to the chair by the bed and he sat down. He held up his cup and then pointed to her. She nodded and mouthed back, "Just black."

Hope was in the kitchen when Father Michael came in. He touched her shoulder, but she pulled away. "Martha's awake. I offered to bring her coffee," he said, filling a cup. "She just wants it black-right?"Hope nodded, but said nothing. She had no plans to talk to him or even look at him.

Still annoyed with her attitude, he resisted continuing last night's argument. Instead he turned and left with the coffee. He would worry about getting back into Hope's good graces later. For now he needed to concentrate on Martha. Maybe he could begin an early morning coffee ritual with her while Hope was busy in the kitchen. It could be an opportunity for him to gradually add a drop of poison to her cup each day, just enough to hasten her decline.

Martha meanwhile was thrilled to have Michael spend more time alone with her. She wanted him completely to herself without Hope hovering around. He took out the chalkboard and described the overnight snowfall and the beauty of the Sutter property in the gleaming white blanket of snow.

Martha responded by asking if the family's old sleigh was still in the barn. She wrote about when she was a girl and the family always celebrated the first big snow with a sleigh ride around the property. Happy times she wrote, smiling.

Father Michael wrote that he hadn't seen the sleigh, but the carriage was still there and in good condition. He suggested selling it to a collector, since they didn't keep horses any longer.

Suddenly Martha's smile faded and her face turned cold and angry. She printed in large letters and mouthed, "NO NEVER! I DON'T WANT TO SELL ANY OF MY THINGS. YOU UNDERSTAND!"

Too late, he realized his mistake and quickly wrote, "I'm sorry Martha. I shouldn't have suggested that. They're your belongings of course." Without looking at him, Martha threw down the chalkboard and angrily waved him away.

Back upstairs in his office, Father Michael looked at his Ways financial ledger. For more than a year without Martha's or Hope's knowledge, he had quietly been selling off the antiques in the barn and the outbuildings. To date, he had collected more than $25,000 from the sales. The sleigh had gone for $2500 to a gentleman farmer outside of town. That same man was also interested in buying the carriage. All these profits were being used to support Ways and its growing membership. He knew he was stealing, but it was for the good of Ways and he planned to never let Martha and Hope know about these sales. Frustrated with himself for angering both women, he knew he had to regain their trust and affections quickly. His plans for obtaining the Sutter property were ruined if he failed.

To clear his head, he pulled on his warm clothes and boots

and went out to plough the driveway and maybe Sutter Court too. All the residents liked it when he used his construction vehicles to help out the neighborhood. Hopefully, he would see Branch or Livy while he was plowing. He couldn't get the police car out of his mind and he desperately needed to find out if it had anything to do with Ways.

()

Chapter 13

Classes started the second week in January at the University. Branch was taking extra courses to try to finish the MBA program early. He and Livy had decided they needed to get away from Oakton and Father Michael's bizarre commune as soon as possible. As he was crossing the campus, he saw Father Michael, dressed in his priest outfit, handing out pamphlets to a group of students.

Branch quickly ducked into the library and out of sight, but Father Michael had already seen him and followed him inside into the lobby. He put his hand on Branch's shoulder. "How's it going man? I haven't seen you or Livy since before Christmas."

"We're doing fine Father Michael. How about you and Hope and your group?"

"It's not a group, Branch. It's called Ways. Remember? Here take some of our pamphlets. I just picked them up from the printer. Some of your fellow students could be interested."

Branch took a few pamphlets and flipped through one. The four color brochure had been done professionally and included pictures of Father Michael conducting evening services, the Sutter Mansion, smiling children and adults sharing a meal, as well as a description of Ways and its history and mission. The last paragraph ended with the tagline, "Shed your loneliness and despair. Come join our family in Ways and realize the dream." The Sutter Court address and contact information bordered the bottom of the pamphlet.

"Very nice. This must have been an expensive print job," Branch commented."I'll show it to Livy. Sorry, but I need to be getting to class."

"Of course," Father Michael said, walking out the door with him. "By the way, I saw a police car pulling away from your house a few nights ago. Did something happen? I mean are you in trouble? Do you need help?"

Branch laughed quietly. "No, we're not in trouble, but someone is. We just don't know who yet. Somehow they got into our house while we were away and went through our things. It looks like they ran out through the basement door when we got home. They also left a strange sadistic gift on our front porch. The police came and they're working on it. The Bakers have added all new locks. We hope that will keep them from coming back."

Father Michael frowned. "That's terrible Branch. Did they steal anything?"

"We haven't missed anything yet. It just seems like they were just creeps enjoying themselves in our house while we were away. The police said that even if nothing was stolen, it's still considered a crime that needs investigating. "

"What was on the front porch?" Father Michael persisted.

Branch couldn't wait to get away from him, so he quickly answered, "Some kind of weird ritualistic offering of dead animals and bones surrounded by antique looking silver candlesticks. All very strange. I really do have to get going now. I'll see you later," he said, hurrying away.

Father Michael watched Branch until he was out of sight. The words "ritualistic offering of dead animals and bones surrounded by antique silver candlesticks" echoed in his brain. Were the police trying to connect Ways to this crime? Is that why they were parked in front of the mansion? He felt exposed and at risk for the first time since arriving in Oakton. He nervously looked around the campus and wondered if he was being watched right now. He put the brochures in his pocket and forced himself to calmly walk to his car.

As he drove back to the mansion, he kept looking through the rear view mirror, but no one seemed to be following him. Maybe he was overreacting. Nevertheless, he was sweating and the hair on the back of his neck stood up while he tried to think of what possible information the police might have to connect him or Ways to the crime. Of course, it was Hope who had told him Branch and Livy were going away. He couldn't remember telling anyone himself, but he wondered if Hope had told someone else. It was another reason she had become a liability and couldn't be trusted. He resolved to talk to the Elders and bring them up to date on his progress and now this possible police investigation. He hoped they would advise him on what he needed to do.

○

chapter 14

Livy and Rory were spending a bitterly, cold and gloomy Sunday afternoon alone at home while Branch was at the library. With the doors locked and double bolted, Livy felt safe there during the day. Nothing strange had happened since that frightening night, but when the doorbell rang, she jumped and cautiously looked through the curtains. Hope was standing there alone shivering on the front porch. Livy quickly unlocked the door and pulled her inside. "My goodness Hope, what are you doing out in the cold without a coat!" she exclaimed. "Sit down while I get a quilt to warm you up."

Hope sagged down into the nearest chair while Livy pulled a quilt out of the bedroom and wrapped her up. Rory had stopped playing with her toys and stared at Hope and then at Livy. "She crying Mama."

"I know honey. Run get some tissues for her, please," Livy said, rubbing Hope's shoulders. "I have hot water on the stove. Would you like some tea?"

Hope nodded and then whispered, "Thank you," to Rory when she gave her the tissue box.

By the time Livy brought the tea in, she found Hope smiling

while Rory was sharing her dolls and their different outfits. The combination of the hot tea and Rory's sweet, comforting, pretend play helped her to recover and she began to relax.

"Did something happen at home?" Livy asked quietly.

Hope stared at the floor. "I just told Aunt Martha that Michael and I are married and we're expecting a baby. I thought she'd be happy to have Michael in the family and to know the Sutter family line would go on for another generation."

Livy sighed. "She wasn't happy?"

Hope shook her head. "I've never seen her so angry. She stood up and signed at me to get out of her sight. She called Michael and me BETRAYERS, before she lost her balance and fell back down into her wheelchair."

"Why would she think you two betrayed her?" Livy asked, gently.

Hope took a deep breath. "Aunt Martha gets confused sometimes. She's been that way for years. From the first day she met Michael, she's had this crazy notion that somehow he is her fiancee who has finally come back to her from World War II. I know that sounds insane and of course impossible, but Michael has sort of encouraged her to believe he has feelings for her. He holds her hand and dotes on her. They write notes to each other. It's really very sweet to see."

Livy gasped. "But why would he do that? She's an elderly woman and he's a young man."

Hope's voice hardened. "He's trying to win her over by playing with her confused emotions because he wants the Sutter property for Ways. At the same time he convinced me that he loved me and wanted to marry me. Now our baby is coming and he's not at all happy about that. I don't think he loves me or cares about Aunt Martha at all. It's all about the property."

"Let me get this straight," Livy said. "Father Michael has been seducing you and courting your aunt at the same time. And now you suspect he's really just after the property. What a jerk! If what you believe is true, he's nothing, but a gold digger and a gigolo!" she snapped.

Hope stood up. "What Michael doesn't understand is that Aunt Martha and I will never let the Sutter property go. It's all we have left in the world. Anyway, Michael apologized to me in a note this morning and said he was going to Boston for a few days. That gives me some time to think about what I should do, but right now, I really should get back to the house. Maybe Aunt Martha has calmed down and we can talk this through."

Livy unlocked the front door. "Let me know if we can help. You must take care of yourself and the baby. You're seeing a doctor aren't you?"

Hope shook her head. "Michael and Ways don't believe in doctors. I plan to find a doctor soon, but I have to keep it a secret from him. Thank you Livy for being my friend," Hope smiled and waved goodbye to Rory, and then almost in an afterthought said, "By the way, why do you have all these new locks?"

"Extra locks are on all our doors now. Someone broke in here while we were away for Christmas," Livy said. "Whoever it was ran out through the basement door when we got home. The police are looking for them, but we haven't heard anything yet. I'm sorry Hope, but they may talk to you about it."

Hope leaned against the door frame for support. "Why would they talk to me?"

"They asked us for the names of anyone we told we were going to be away. I remembered telling you. I suppose they'll ask you who you might have told. Mr. Baker thinks it could have been one of the strangers who are attending Ways services."

"Oh, I don't think so. They're all nice people," Hope mumbled, walking away. "The Bakers just don't like us."

Branch drove up at the same time and waved to Hope, but she kept walking away with her head down and didn't return his wave. He ran up the walk to the porch, kissed Livy and pointed to Hope. "What was that all about?" he asked, taking off his coat and putting his baseball cap on Rory.

Branch shook his head after Livy told him Hope's news and her beliefs about Father Michael's motives. "That's a crazy story. Look, Father Michael is a strange guy, but I can't believe he would do something so underhanded. He's running Ways which means he's in charge of the lives of at least a hundred people. And he's recruiting more members all the time. Plus he's constantly working on the Sutter property and taking on other contract construction jobs to raise extra money. You're saying Hope believes he still had the time to seduce and marry her AND court Martha Sutter . The man must be exhausted!" Branch laughed.

Livy shrugged. "I believe her. Maybe he's gone away to give Martha and Hope time to miss him and need him even more. Does he have family in Boston?"

"I don't know, but I think he told me there's a Ways connection in Massachusetts," Branch answered. "He may have gone there for help or advice. I wonder who's in charge of the commune while he's gone."

"There's one more thing," Livy said. "Hope asked about the extra locks and I told her about someone being in here while we were gone. She seemed very nervous that the police might talk to her. That's probably why she didn't want to talk to you."

Branch started pacing around the room. "That's funny, because Father Michael had the same reaction when I told him what had happened. Makes me wonder if they've known about it all along. If Hope used to live in this house, she might still have keys that fit the old locks. Maybe the two of them decided to make themselves at home here while we were gone."

"No, I won't believe that!" Livy gasped. "Hope was so upset when she got here. I wasn't even thinking of telling her about what happened over Christmas, but then she noticed the new locks. Oh Branch, I hate this! What if you're right? What if she's been sneaking in here with an old set of keys the whole time we've been here?"

Branch put his arm around her. "Don't you think we would have noticed if someone had been in here over the last few months? Let's ask the Bakers how many sets of keys Martha and Hope turned over to them when they bought the house. The police might be interested in knowing before they talk to Hope and Father Michael."

()

Chapter 15

Hope went straight to the solarium when she got back to the house. Martha was sitting in her wheelchair among the pink and white flowering tropical plants. She had picked a few of the blossoms and was rubbing them between the palms of her hands. She flinched when Hope touched her shoulder.

"I'm sorry Aunt Martha. I never meant to hurt you when I told you about Michael and me. Please forgive me," she signed. "I realize now I should never have married Michael. All he really wants is to get the Sutter property away from us for Ways. That's why he's so sweet to you, and he thinks I will help him do that because as his wife, I'm supposed to obey him in all things. It's an evil plan, but you must believe me, I will never let him hurt you."

Martha stared at Hope with tired eyes and held up her hand to stop her frantic signing. "Thank you for telling me. I need to think about what you said. I've been such an old fool. Come back later and we'll talk," she signed.

Hope smiled and nodded. She felt a calmness settling over her. She and Aunt Martha would find a way to deal with Michael. For now she was relieved he had gone away. As she passed through the front foyer, she met Walter Kelly coming out of the dining room. He was Father Michael's main assistant in Ways. A quiet, well mannered, young man with long brown hair swept back in a ponytail, he had dropped out of the University when Father Michael met him and brought him into the commune. After a few months of training, Father Michael was able to rely on Walter to take charge whenever he wasn't around.

"I was coming to find you Hope," Walter said in a rush. "You need to come with me. Mary has gone into labor over in the barn, and she won't let anyone help her."

Hope grabbed her coat. "Which one is Mary?"

"She and her children live in one of the outbuildings. Please hurry. She seems in very bad shape," Walter emphasized.

"Who's the father? Is he with her?" Hope asked before they reached the barn.

Walter stopped. "I don't know who the father is. Mary came here alone with the children a while back. Father Michael has been looking after her ever since."

Hope kept walking, but she silently wondered if Michael was the father. That would have been part of his way of looking after her. "Let's try to move her to her quarters. The barn is no place to have a baby. Besides you'll be wanting to get set up for evening services soon."

Mary was lying on two benches pulled together with a jacket under her head for a pillow. The color had drained from her face and her long black hair and clothes were soaked with sweat. Her contractions were erratic and violent. She thrashed out at anyone who came near her and kept crying out for Father Michael. Her two young children were staring at her and crying too.

Hope took Mary's hand and spoke quietly. "It's Hope, Father Michael's wife. He's not here now, but Walter and I are going to help you. We're going to move you to your quarters. You'll be more comfortable there. These women will stay here with your children." She motioned to Walter. "Help me get her up and we'll try to walk her to her room. Come on Mary, let's get you into your comfortable bed."

Between the two of them, they half walked and carried Mary to the outbuilding next to the barn, but they couldn't get her up the stairs to the bedroom. As soon as they laid her down on the couch, she writhed in pain with another contraction. Hope looked at Walter who was backing out the door. "Have you helped Father Michael with delivering babies here?"

Walter's face was white and he shook his head. "Never! I wouldn't know what to do. I can't do this."

Hope grabbed his arm. "I've never done this either, but we're going to have to. There's no one else here. Ask one of the other mothers to come help us. At least she will know what it's like to have a baby. Hurry!"

"Maybe we should call for a doctor or an ambulance and send her to the hospital, "Walter gasped.

Hope shook her head. "Father Michael would never permit outside help to come in here. You know how strict he is about that. Now please hurry and bring over one of the mothers."

Mary's labor went on through the night and into the next morning. The contractions became stronger and closer together. But when it was time to push, the lifeless baby boy came out feet first with the cord tightly wrapped around his neck. Hope couldn't stop the enormous amount of blood flowing out of Mary. She lost consciousness and stopped breathing. After all the violence of the birth, the room became utterly still and no one moved. Eventually, Walter took a blanket and covered both Mary and the baby. Hope wiped her hands on a towel and thanked the mother who had tried to help. Then she asked Walter to tell the men to dig another grave in the Sutter cemetery.

"What about Mary's other children?" Walter asked.

"The commune women will take care of them. Ways is one big happy family, remember?" Hope answered wearily.

The mansion was quiet when Hope came in from the barn. She went to her room, changed out of her bloody clothes, and washed her hands and face. She hurried to the kitchen to prepare breakfast for the Ways who would be coming in soon. Finally, she poured coffee for herself and one for Martha.

Martha was still in her clothes from the day before. "Where were you last night?" she angrily signed. "I had no dinner and I had to sleep in my clothes."

"I'm sorry Aunt Martha. I meant to come back, but one of the women in the commune went into labor last night. Michael is away for a few days, so I tried to do what I could for her, but I failed everyone. Both she and the baby died," Hope signed.

Martha reached for Hope's hand. "I'm sorry," she mouthed and then signed. "It's not fair for you to have to care for these strangers. You don't know anything about delivering babies. Why didn't you call an ambulance?"

"You already know why. Michael's rule is no interference in Ways from outsiders. He doesn't want anyone to know what's happening here. We're supposed to take care of everything ourselves, including medical care," Hope signed.

Martha shook her head and her fingers furiously signed, "That poor girl should have been in the hospital. Now she and her baby are dead on my land. We're all responsible if the police find out."

Hope tried to calm her down. "Don't worry Aunt Martha. I told the men to bury them in the cemetery. As Michael says, "What happens in Ways stays in Ways. No one else will know. But for me, one thing is certain. After what I saw happen to that girl, I'm going to see a doctor and I'm having my baby in the hospital. Even Michael won't be able to stop me."

◯

chapter 16

Father Michael felt calmer in Boston. He realized how entrenched he had become with the Ways commune in Oakton. His messy entanglements with the Sutter women were strangling his progress with the mission and business of Ways. At times he had found himself longing to be free and alone. As he waited for his meeting with Bishop John and the other Ways Elders, he prayed they could offer him strength to continue.

Bishop John studied Father Michael's face with the dark circles under his eyes and embraced him. "You look so tired. Is something wrong?"

Father Michael exhaled. "The last few weeks have been exhausting, and I haven't been sleeping well. I didn't realize how difficult this assignment would be."

"Are the members giving you trouble?" Brother Phillip asked.

"No more than usual. They're a good group, very committed to Ways and the future it offers them. We have about two hundred and fifty members who attend services regularly. Of course for now, we only have enough room to house twenty adults and children. The others are still living off site. It's the Sutter women I'm having trouble controlling," Father Michael fumed.

"What's the problem?" Brother Paul asked.

"As you know, Hope has been my wife for more than a year. At first she was very loving and agreeable with the rules of Ways and my relationships with the other women in the commune. She obeyed me without question. But lately, she has begun questioning everything I do and she disobeys me. She's locked me out of our bedroom and won't talk to me. Worst of all she's pregnant with our child," Father Michael explained.

Bishop John smiled. "But this news of a child for you is wonderful my son. Why do you think it's such a bad thing? The more children you bring into Ways, all the better. They're the easiest ones to train to follow our teachings without question. This child will be ours. Hope is just a vessel."

Father Michael looked down. "I know I should be happy about this baby, but what you don't know, and what I didn't know when I convinced her to marry me is this deafness in her family is hereditary. It's called Meniere's Disease and there's no cure. It usually doesn't start until after age forty, so Hope has no symptoms yet. Her father had it before he died and her Aunt Martha has it. Plus Hope's mother was a deaf mute from birth. I think it's very possible this baby could inherit deafness one way or another, even if Hope never develops it. She should have warned me. I am against bringing another person into the world with a hereditary disease."

Bishop John and the Elders exchanged worried looks. "You're going to have to put aside all your marital issues and convince Hope that you love her and you're happy about the baby. Besides it could be years before you know if this disease has been passed on. Meanwhile the success of Ways in Oakton is what's most important.

What's going on with Martha Sutter? We thought you had a positive relationship with her."

Father Michael nodded. "It's true. We've become very friendly. I thought she completely trusted me and my ability to manage her property. But I foolishly suggested selling some of her antiques, and she became very angry. She told me she has no intention of letting go of any family property ever, not to me or anyone else. Then she told me to leave."

"So your original plan of eventually gaining ownership of the Sutter property for Ways was by marrying Hope. You believe she will inherit everything from Martha, and it will then become yours because she is your wife. Are you saying that plan is in jeopardy?" Brother Paul asked.

Father Michael sighed. "I'm afraid so. But I can still get the property if I do what you said Bishop John. I have to convince Hope that I love her and need her and I'm happy about the baby. At the same time, I'll try to smooth over my relationship with Martha and then begin giving her tiny untraceable amounts of poison every day."

"You've talked about this before. Are you certain you can do this ? Where would you get such a lethal substance?" Brother Paul asked.

"I have a lot of different chemicals I use for cleaning and landscaping. If that doesn't work, I know some of the hippies at the University who use drugs regularly. I should be able to get something from them." Father Michael paused.

"Just don't draw attention to yourself or to Ways," Brother Phillip warned. "The last thing we need are the police investigating our organization and all the negative publicity that would cause."

Bishop John agreed. "This is very important Father Michael. Of course, we will continue to underwrite your Sutter commune, but you must not lose sight of our larger mission to expand Ways by acquiring potentially valuable property and making every location a financially independent operation which regularly contributes to our ruling Boston Board. Any kind of suspicion about your location would slow us down. We might even be forced to abandon the Oakton commune and move the members to other locations. In the past, it's happened to other communes and cults. We don't want Oakton to become another one."

Father Michael stood up and put his hand over his heart. "On my life, I swear I will work things out. I won't let the Oakton commune fail."

Bishop John and the two Elders stood up too and placed their hands on Father Michael's hand. "We have your word. Keep us informed, " Bishop John said.

()

Chapter 17

Officers Williams and Holmes drove up the driveway to the Sutter mansion. Several weeks had passed since they had been called to Branch and Livy Monroe's house to investigate the strange burglary. During that time they had interviewed most of the people who had known the Monroes were away. Nothing unusual had turned up so far, and none of the unknown fingerprints found in the house had matched any of their criminal files. Today they were hoping to talk to Hope Sutter Brown.

At the door, Officer Holmes pointed to the Medusa door knocker. "Look at this. What do you think that means?"

"I don't know," Officer Williams laughed. "Maybe it's to scare people away. Let's give it a try," he said, knocking on the door.

When the Medusa face slid open, a woman's voice asked if she could help them. "Are you Hope Sutter Brown?" Officer Williams asked.

"Yes, who's asking?" Hope answered.

Officer Williams and Officer Holmes introduced themselves and held their identifications up to the opening. "We just want to talk to you about a burglary that happened on your street a few weeks ago," Officer Williams said.

Hope opened the door and the officers stepped in. "We can sit in here," she said, leading them into the dining room. "Is this about what happened at the Monroes'? Livy just told me the other day you might be coming to see me."

"So you already know about it?" Officer Holmes asked.

Hope started nervously clasping and unclasping her fingers. "Just what she told me."

"Do you have any idea who might have done that?" Officer Williams asked.

"Of course not," Hope answered.

"But you knew the Monroes were going away," Officer Williams continued.

Hope kept fidgeting. "Yes, Livy told me, but I wasn't sure when they were coming back."

"Did you notice anyone around their house while they were gone?" Officer Holmes asked.

"No, why would I?" she answered.

"Do you remember telling anyone the Monroes were going away?" Officer Williams asked.

Hope frowned. "I told my husband Michael. He had suggested we invite them to Christmas dinner. I can't think of anyone else."

"Is he here? We'd like to talk to him," Officer Williams followed up.

"He's in Boston on business right now. He should be home in a day or so. If there's nothing else, I need to check on my elderly aunt. I look after her. She's an invalid," Hope said, standing up.

"Just one more thing," Officer Williams continued. "We

understand you have boarders living here. Is that right?"

Hope frowned again. "Not really. We 're a spiritual group here. Our members don't pay for their rooms. We think of them as family, not boarders. They contribute what they can."

"Any chance one of them may have heard you tell your husband the Monroes would be away?" he asked.

Hope shook her head. "I don't think so, but I suppose it's possible."

"Are there other members of your group who don't live here on the property?" Officer Holmes asked.

Hope nodded. "Yes, we have a number of members who come here for evening services, but they have to live elsewhere for now. We're planning to add more living quarters in the future."

"Who's in charge of your community?"Officer Holmes asked.

"My husband Michael is the leader," she answered.

"You said he'd be home soon. Please let him know we need to talk to him. We'll stop back by in a few days," he said.

The Officers stood up and handed Hope their cards. "Thank you Mrs. Brown. If you think of anything else that might help us, please let us know," Officer Williams said, as Hope led them to the door. "By the way, did you happen to tell your aunt the Monroes were away?"

Hope opened the door. "Why would I tell her? I told you she's an invalid and she's deaf. All our conversations are in sign language. Besides, she doesn't know the Monroes," she said, closing the door after them. For a few minutes, she leaned heavily against the door. Her heart was racing and she felt dizzy and afraid. As angry as she was with Michael, she wished he was here with her now.

Officers Williams and Holmes pulled out of the driveway and parked down the street to discuss Hope's interview. "What do you think?" Officer Williams asked, after they compared their notes.

Officer Holmes shook his head. "She seemed very nervous and she really wanted us to leave."

Officer Williams started the car and pulled away. "I think she knows a lot more than she told us. We need to talk to her husband. Did you notice the silver candlesticks on the table? They look like the ones we took from the Monroes' front porch. Maybe that's a coincidence or maybe not."

As they turned off Sutter Court, a taxi passed them heading up the street toward the mansion with Father Michael in the back seat. When he saw the police car, he immediately slid down in the seat away from the windows. Bishop John's warning filled his ears. "Don't draw attention to yourself or Ways. The last thing we need is a police investigation or negative publicity about our organization."

Father Michael shivered and thought, "It's too late. The police are already looking at us."

Hope saw the taxi coming up the driveway. When Father Michael came up the front steps, she opened the door and put her arms around him. "Thank goodness you're back. We have to talk."

"I know," he whispered and followed her upstairs to their bedroom. He put his arms around her and hugged her tightly. "I'm sorry I got upset with you about the baby. I'll never hurt you again. I promise. I've had time to think about everything and I do want our child. We must pray every day that you and this child will remain healthy and the Meniere's Disease will not be passed on. If what you say stays true, the disease won't start until between the ages of forty and sixty. We'll have years to enjoy this child and he or she won't have to worry about it for a very long time. For now, I'm more worried about you."

Hope smiled. "Thank you Michael. I forgive you. You'll be a wonderful father. But right now I need to talk to you about two things that happened while you were away."

Father Michael put his hand up before she could continue. "I saw a police car pulling out of our street. Were they here?"

Hope nodded. "They're investigating the break in at Branch and Livy's house. They wanted to know if I told anyone about the Monroes being away over Christmas."

Father Michael frowned. "Did you tell them anything?"

"I told them you were the only one I could remember telling. Then they asked me how many other people live here besides Aunt Martha. They called them boarders and seemed to think one of them might have overheard me telling you about the Monroes being away."

Father Michael laughed and looked relieved. "So they think we're running a boarding house?"

Hope looked down. "Not exactly. I explained that we're a spiritual community. I told them some members live here and others come for evening services."

"Oh Hope, why did you say that?" Father Michael groaned. "So now thanks to you, they probably suspect we're a commune. Did they ask about me?"

Hope nodded. "I'm sorry Michael. They wanted to know who the leader is and I told them you are. They're coming back to talk to you."

"I'm not surprised, "Father Michael grumbled. "But they'll have a hard time connecting any of our members to that crime. What we really have to worry about are the suspicions they may have about Ways and our communal life here."

Hope sighed. "Michael, there's something else that happened while you were gone." He stared quietly at her while she described how Mary had gone into labor, and that she and Walter and one of the other Ways women tried to help her. "We did all we could for her, but we didn't know what we were doing and we couldn't save them. The baby boy was born dead and Mary died too. Walter and some of the other men buried them together in the cemetery. We didn't know what else to do," she cried.

Father Michael's voice was hoarse. "Mary was such a sweet person. You know I was looking after her and the two girls. I'll never forgive myself for not being here for her when she needed me the most. And now I've lost her and this baby boy."

Before she could stop herself, Hope blurted out, "Was this your baby, Michael?"

He stared at her."Of course he was. All the children in Ways belong to all the members. It doesn't matter who conceived them. It will be the same for the baby you're carrying. You know this is one of our covenants."

Hope shook her head, but he ignored her and kept talking. "Look Hope, I'm not going to waste time arguing with you about this because you know I'm right. We have to concentrate on preserving our Ways community and giving the police as little information as possible. I need to talk to Walter and look at that new grave. We can't let the police find it. We may need to move their bodies to the mausoleum," he said, leaving the room.

After Michael left to find Walter, Hope sat very still thinking about her husband's words. Then she went to the end of the long hallway and looked out the back window. She saw Michael and Walter walking into the tall grass in the cemetery and down the sloping hill to the edge of the woods. They stopped there and Walter pointed at the ground. Michael was talking and gesturing. Afterwards they walked back up the hill and stopped at the mausoleum and talked some more.

Hope turned away. "Damn you Michael. Aunt Martha and I will make sure you never get this baby for Ways, and the Sutter property will never be yours either. We will be rid of you and Ways forever," she whispered.

()

Chapter 18

Except for occasionally exchanging waves, Branch and Livy didn't see the Bakers until the end of January when it was time to pay their rent. On Saturday morning, Branch went next door with the check. As usual they welcomed him and asked him to sit down. "How's the new semester going?" Georgia asked.

"It's keeping me busy," Branch smiled. "I'm taking extra courses so I can finish all the class work by this summer. I don't have to be on campus while I'm writing my thesis. I'll find a job so Livy and I can move on as soon as possible."

"You'll be leaving us so soon?" Ed asked

"That's right. We hope so, but of course we'll let you know in plenty of time, so you can advertise for new tenants," Branch answered.

Georgia shook her head. "But we don't want new tenants. We want you to stay. You could buy the house from us. Why can't you look for a job here? TVA isn't far away and they're always hiring smart people like you. Ed, you could introduce him to the right people couldn't you?" she pleaded.

"I'd be glad to do that if you're interested," Ed agreed.

Branch hadn't expected this reaction from the Bakers and

he hesitated before he answered. "Thank you very much. That would be wonderful, but of course, I have to talk to Livy. We're still not over what happened during Christmas week. Every little creak makes us think someone else is in the house. We haven't heard anything from the police either. You'd think they would tell us what's going on. Have you heard from them?"

"Not a word. Ed was thinking of giving them a call to see if they've found out anything," Georgia said.

"I was thinking of doing the same thing, but I wanted to talk to you first. Livy and I were wondering if Hope might have kept a set of keys to our house after Martha sold it to you. You didn't change the locks then, did you?" Branch asked.

Ed's face turned red. "Martha and Hope gave us two sets of old keys. You have one and we kept one. I suppose it's possible there are other duplicates. I never thought to ask them. I didn't have the locks changed because I love those beautiful doors and the old fashioned locks. They go with the house."

"Do you think Hope had extra keys and stayed in your house while you were gone? She's such a sweet woman. I can't imagine her doing something like that!" Georgia exclaimed.

"No, we don't think it was her," Branch said quickly. "But if she did have extra keys, someone else up there at the house might have used them."

Ed grunted. "I wouldn't put it past that Father Michael. He's a real charmer. If Hope's really his wife now, he can probably convince her to do anything he wants, including breaking the law."

Branch stood up to leave. "I'm sorry I brought this up. I can see I've upset you both. I think I'll mention the keys to the police when I talk to them. Thank you for offering to help me find a job. That's very kind of you. I'll let you know what we decide."

Georgia and Ed both smiled. "It's our pleasure. Please think about staying," she said.

Livy's reaction to the Bakers' offer was swift. "Absolutely not! We're not staying in this dangerous house on this crazy street one minute longer than we have to. Even if you got an amazing job offer around here and you took it, we'd have to move away from Sutter Court and Ways. The Bakers are nice people, but they can't expect us to be their buffer against Father Michael and his spiritualists forever."

"I know, honey. I don't want to live here either. I'm just surprised they thought we would even consider this small cottage as our permanent home. We'll stick to our plan and leave as soon as the semester is over," Branch reassured her.

Livy nodded, but she couldn't let go of the impossible idea of staying. "How could they think we would consider bringing up Rory next to a commune? Those children up there already have different ideas and expectations. We can't let her associate with them. Who knows what kind of physical and mental abuse they may be subjected to on a daily basis? And don't forget that cemetery and those disturbed graves. We have to get out of here!"

"Take it easy! It's only for a few more months and then we'll leave," Branch promised.

"What did the Bakers say about the keys to the house?" Livy asked.

Branch exhaled. "They seemed surprised at the idea that Martha and Hope might have duplicate keys. Georgia said she couldn't imagine Hope coming in here if we weren't home. But Ed said he wouldn't put it past Father Michael. I'm going to go ahead and call Officer Williams or Officer Holmes and see what's going on."

Livy pursed her lips. "I wonder if they've talked to Hope and Father Michael yet."

()

Chapter 19

Officer Williams reported that they hadn't found any new information on the case, when Branch called him. "We're going up to the Sutter place today to talk to Michael Brown. We spoke to his wife a few days ago, but he was out of town at the time. One thing we noticed was those antique silver candlesticks we took from your porch look like the ones in the Sutter dining room. Have you seen them there?"

"We've never been in that house," Branch answered. "Look Officer, this may not be important, but Livy and I thought of something. Martha Sutter is the original owner of our house. She used to live here and so did her niece Hope, Father Michael's wife. Martha eventually sold the house to our landlords the Bakers. We rented it from them in late August. We've been wondering if Martha and Hope might still have extra keys to our house. Mr. Baker remembers they gave him two sets of keys at the real estate closing. He assumed there weren't others, but here's the thing. He never changed the locks on our house."

"That's interesting," Officer Williams said. "So you think someone else may have duplicate keys and could have used them to enter your house."

"Isn't it possible?" Branch asked.

"Maybe so. We'll see if we can find out about extra keys when we go to the house today. You have new locks now, right?" he asked.

"Yes, we have additional ones. Mr. Baker didn't want to change out the antique ones. We have new dead bolts everywhere," Branch laughed.

"We'll let you know if we find out anything. Thanks for calling Branch," Officer Williams said and hung up.

The Officers drove up to the Sutter house in the early afternoon. Dressed in his priest outfit, Father Michael was working on the front loader when they arrived. "Can I help you?" he asked, when they got out of the car.

The Officers introduced themselves and asked if he was Michael Brown. "Yes, I'm Father Michael," he smiled. "My wife told me you were here the other day. What can I do for you?"

"Are you a priest?" Officer Williams asked.

"I'm the leader of a spiritual community here. I choose to wear these clothes as a sign of commitment to the members and to our beliefs."

"But you're not an ordained Catholic priest or a member of the Protestant clergy. What's the name of your organization?" Officer Williams continued.

Father Michael smiled again. "We're a branch of a very old spiritual community dating back to colonial times called Ways. There are other branches in different places across the country. Are you here to learn about our organization?"

Officer Williams shook his head. "Actually no. We're

investigating a burglary on your street. It happened during the week between Christmas and New Year's. We wondered if you'd heard anything about it."

"You're talking about the Monroes' house over there," Father Michael pointed.

"That's right. You know them?" Officer Holmes asked.

Father Michael nodded. "They're good people. Branch told me about what happened and Livy told my wife. It's a shame. This is such a quiet street. You don't expect something like that to happen."

"Did you know they were away?" Officer Holmes continued. Father Michael nodded and explained that both he and Hope knew.

"How many members do you have here in Ways?" Officer Williams asked.

"We have around two hundred fifty active members who attend evening services regularly. But I'm not aware that any of them know who the Monroes are or where they live, if that's what you want to know," Father Michael answered.

Both officers turned and looked at the mansion. "You can't possibly have that many people living here!" Officer Williams exclaimed.

Father Michael smiled. "No, of course not. We only have room to house twenty adults and children here on the property. Hopefully, someday we'll be able to accommodate everyone. At least that's our goal."

"So other members come and go on a regular basis?" Officer Williams asked.

"That's right," he answered. "It's not ideal, but it's working so far."

"So let me get this straight. Every night approximately two hundred thirty people walk or drive up and down Sutter Court and pass the Monroes' house. Is that right?" Officer Holmes asked.

Father Michael was becoming uneasy with all the questions, but he tried to calm his nerves and hide it from the officers. "Well, not everyone is able to attend every single night. Some of our members have jobs outside the commune. Others are going to the University full-time. But yes, we require all members to attend nightly and most do. If they don't comply, they have to confess the reason."

Officer Williams frowned. "We'd like to look around. Would you mind showing us where you hold your meetings?"

Father Michael shrugged. "I don't mind at all, but our members begin arriving around 4:00. I'd need to complete your tour before then."

The Officers and Father Michael walked past the mansion and across to the large barn. Inside on a cobblestone floor, rows of benches formed a semicircle facing a pulpit. Soft lighting and the whir of several space heaters made the open area feel warm and comforting. Several women were covering long tables with burgundy cloths set across the back wall, while young children played around them. The old horse stalls along two walls were being used for kitchen space and storage. A bathroom with several stalls occupied a corner next to a set of narrow stairs leading to the upper loft.

"What's up there?" Officer Holmes asked.

"Some of our members sleep up there. It's a dormitory-like setting with cots in curtained off spaces for privacy and there's another bathroom with shower stalls," Father Michael answered.

"We're very proud of how we've been able to reconfigure this barn space to suit our needs. Our members feel comfortable and at home here."

Outside, Father Michael pointed to the outbuildings. "We've been able to convert these buildings into small communal units for families. It's our plan to add on to these structures in the future to offer more living spaces."

Officer Williams shielded his eyes and squinted. "Is that a cemetery over there in back of the house?"

Father Michael sighed. "That's the Sutter family cemetery. It's been untended for years. So it's in very bad shape. Miss Sutter, the owner and our landlord, doesn't want us to clean it up. We have to respect her wishes of course, and we try to keep our members away from it."

"So it's not in use?" Officer Holmes asked.

"No one has been in there in years as far as I know. It's beginning to get dark, Officers. If there's nothing else, our members will be arriving soon. I need to prepare for evening services."

The Officers shook Father Michael's hand and gave him their cards. "Thank you for your time. Call us if you think of anything that would be helpful to our investigation," Officer Williams said. "By the way, is Mrs. Brown home? There's something we didn't ask her the other day."

"I'm sure she told you everything she knows. Do you really need to talk to her again?" Father Michael asked.

"It won't take long. Is she here?" he asked again.

Annoyed, Father Michael led them into the foyer of the house. "Wait here. I'll see if I can find her."

A few minutes later, Hope, wearing an apron and drying her hands on a towel appeared with Father Michael. "Sorry to bother you again, Mrs. Brown. We just have one quick question," Officer Williams apologized. "We understand you and your aunt both lived in the Monroe house before she sold it to the present owners, the Bakers. Is that right?"

Hope nodded. "Yes, that's true. Why?"

"When the house was sold, did you and your aunt turn over all your keys and any duplicates to the Bakers?" he continued.

Surprised by the question, Hope's face flushed and she looked at Michael. "We both gave them our keys," she stammered. "That's all I know."

Father Michael put his arm around Hope. "I think we've answered your questions, Officers. We really need to prepare for evening services."

"Yes, thank you for your time," Officer Williams said, as they turned and left the house. As the Officers drove down Sutter Court, they noticed men and women with small children walking up the street toward the mansion.

"Here they come just like he said. Look at them all and this happens every night!" Officer Holmes exclaimed. "It's like an invasion. Hard to believe no one has complained about this!"

()

Chapter 20

The red stinging rash on Martha's hands had eased. Now she was wearing gloves when she picked the Oleander blossoms with their stems and leaves and then carefully mashed them into tiny poisonous drops of juice which she collected in a jar. It was barely a small trickle of liquid, but she believed it was enough, if given over time, to be lethal. To be safe, she kept the jar with a tight lid hidden in an inside pocket of her wheelchair.

She smiled to herself thinking of her father Abel who, years before, had brought the small Oleander bushes back from Texas after one of his business trips. The tiny pink and white blossoms that looked like delicate periwinkles captivated her. She planted them in pots in the solarium, and over the years they multiplied and grew into tall elegant, treelike bushes, some well over six feet tall. Now they filled the south facing glass wall and bloomed year round.

"Be careful with these special plants, my girl," he had warned. "They originated in ancient Greece and Northern Africa. Sometime around 1841, they were brought to Galveston and now they are flourishing across the deep South. They reminded me of you—delicately beautiful, but dangerous," he laughed and then shared the Oleander legend.

"In Greek mythology, Oleander meant romance and charm and eventual death. The story was about a beautiful Greek maiden who was courted by a young man named Leander who swam across the Hellespont every night to see her. Sadly, one night he drowned in a storm and his name became the mournful sigh, O(h) Leander."

Martha had clapped her hands and hugged her father. "Thank you Papa. I love them!"

"Just the same, my girl, remember this. They say the whole plant is poisonous and can cause death. So love its beauty, but respect its deadly charm. Wash your hands after you handle it and don't let any part of it get into your mouth or eyes," he cautioned.

Now Martha's plan was for Michael to experience the meaning of Oleander. She had made up with him as soon as he returned from his trip. He was so charming and sweet, it was easy to pretend to forgive him. Right away he began bringing her the morning coffee, and she invited him to have a late afternoon glass of sherry with her before Hope brought in her dinner. At most of these times, she would ask him to get something for her from another part of the house and before he came back, she discreetly added tiny drops of the Oleander to his drinks.

Martha had already prepared their drinks when Father Michael arrived for their time that afternoon. He started their chalkboard conversation with, "Sorry I'm late. Busy afternoon. I can't stay long."

"What kept you?" Martha wrote.

Father Michael frowned. "The police were here."

Martha put her hand over her forehead. "Is this about

that poor woman and her baby who died?" she scribbled.

Caught by surprise at her question, he took a long drink of his sherry. "You know about that?" he asked.

Martha bowed her head and nodded. "Did they find the grave?"

"No! No! That's not why they were here," he wrote and then drained his sherry glass. "Hope can explain better than I can. She'll be coming in soon. I have to get over to the barn." He stood up, patted her shoulder and kissed her hand before rushing away. But as he hurried through the sitting room, a nauseating wave of dizziness caused him to lose his balance and he fell onto one of the settees. His last thought before darkness washed over him was, "Damn! I drank the sherry too fast."

Hope had doubted her Aunt Martha would be able to bring herself to actually harm Michael, but when she found him slumped down on the settee, she guessed that the older woman's poison plan was in motion. Suddenly afraid, she shook his shoulder and called his name. "Michael! You need to wake up. You're missing evening services. Everyone is waiting. What's wrong? Are you sick?"

He opened his eyes and looked at her with a blank stare. "I'm just so tired," he mumbled hoarsely and closed his eyes again. "Can't get up now. Tell Walter to go ahead."

Hope hurried out to the barn and found Walter greeting some late comers at the door. "Where's Father Michael?" he asked

"He's not feeling well. He wants you to lead the services tonight, just like you did when he was away," she panted.

"I can do that, but the members get anxious when Father Michael isn't here. Is he all right?" Walter worried.

Hope frowned. "I hope so. He's resting right now. Maybe

he caught something on his trip," she answered and hurried back to the house. She picked up Martha's dinner tray and went to the solarium. When she passed through the sitting room, she found Michael still motionless in a deep sleep.

"You're late. What's going on?" Martha signed.

"I'm sorry," Hope signed. "Michael fell asleep in the sitting room. I tried to wake him up, but he couldn't get up or stay awake. I had to go out to the barn and ask Walter to lead the services. Did you have sherry time with him earlier?"

Martha nodded. "He didn't stay long. He was in a hurry to get to his people in the barn. Said the police had been here and you would tell me why."

"But he seemed all right while he was here?" Hope asked.

Martha nodded again and signed, "We had our sherry and he left. Why were the police here?"

Hope explained about the break in at the cottage during Christmas week. "Branch and Livy had told the police Michael and I knew they would be away. The police wanted to know if we had told anyone else."

"Did you tell anyone?" Martha asked.

Hope shook her head. "Of course not. But the police also wanted to know if you and I had turned over all the keys to the cottage to the Bakers when you sold it."

Martha shrugged. "I guess there could be more keys around here somewhere. I don't know. Do you?"

Hope agreed. "You and I gave the Bakers the keys we had. There's so much stuff in this house and lots of extra keys to who knows what."

Martha franticly signed. "Michael said he kept them away from my cemetery. Do you believe him?"

Hope nodded. "I'm certain he did, but those officers are curious about Ways and what's going on here. I'm afraid we have to worry about them talking to the members and asking questions. One or more of the Ways who know what happened to Mary and the baby might break the commune's strict code of silence."

Hope's words brought Martha close to a panic and she again franticly signed, "This is all my fault. I should never have trusted Michael. I let him live here and bring in all these people. AND YOU—YOU MARRIED HIM! We have to get rid of him and all of them as soon as possible."

Hope stared at her aunt. "You've already started with the poison haven't you? He's already getting sick isn't he?"

Martha sighed. "I have to do this and you have to help me. We're the last of the Sutter family. If we don't, he and Ways will get rid of us."

()

Chapter 21

At police headquarters, Officers Williams and Holmes again compared their notes from the Hope and Father Michael Brown interviews. They agreed the couple had been cooperative, but their answers to many of the questions had only created more troubling suspicions. It did seem, as Branch Monroe had suggested, that Hope and Martha Sutter might still have keys to the Monroe house. And if the aunt was an invalid and never left the house, that meant Hope and Father Michael or someone else from the commune might have used the extra duplicate keys to enter the house. But that didn't explain why they chose to go in there, especially since the Monroes hadn't found anything stolen.

What was most surprising, was that the interviews with the Browns about the mysterious burglary had uncovered a much more complex, possibly criminal situation, and that needed further investigation. It appeared that an active commune called Ways with hundreds of members had secretly been established in Oakton on the Sutter property. They briefed their Captain on the new finding, and he agreed they needed to expand their investigation. The idea that a commune or possibly a cult was underway in Oakton was potentially dangerous for the whole town. The Captain called in

Detectives Moore and Talbot, the only two detectives on the small force, and assigned them to work with Officers Williams and Holmes on the case. After they were fully briefed, the detectives would assume responsibility for the investigation.

To start, the detectives decided to find out more about the Ways organization. If it was true that other settlements existed in the United States, they wanted to know if any crimes or complaints had been associated with them. Secondly, they wanted to know if the Oakton Building Department had any record of the change in the designation of the Sutter property from single family to multi-family. In addition, had building permits been granted for the conversion of the barn to a meeting hall with a dormitory and for the outbuildings to become residences? Lastly, was Children's Services aware of the number of children living there? Were they being properly cared for and enrolled in school if they were old enough? And what about the University? Were they aware of students who may have become involved or were possibly living with Ways?

Detective Moore began researching the Ways organization, while Detective Talbot focused on the various town departments. It didn't take long for Detective Moore to find historical mention of Ways as one of the early experiments in communal living during colonial times. It seemed to have thrived originally as a rejection of organized rigid religion by unhappy churchgoers in favor of a family based community of sharing all monetary assets, as well as living quarters, food, and eventually sexual partners and children. At times Ways was forced to abandon settlements and move its members to new locations after being driven away by the traditional organized churches. For long periods of time, they seemed to disappear completely from historical accounts, but then would later emerge in a different, generally rural part of the country.

In recent years, Detective Moore found references to Ways settlements in Northern California, Washington and Oregon, but no reported criminal activity was noted. Curiously, there was no mention of the Boston area, even though Hope Brown had told the police officers Father Michael had gone there on business. One article about summer farm stands in Massachusetts briefly described one in the Berkshires operated by a hippie community, but no name was mentioned.

Meanwhile, Detective Talbot checked with the town building department. He found no record of requests for building permits on the Sutter property in recent years. Nor was there an application for a zoning change from a single family home to a multifamily complex. The Board of Education had no enrollment records for children from the Sutter address, and the Health Department, as well as Children's Services were not aware of any children currently living there.

The University administrators had no record of students residing on Sutter Court, but reminded the detective that students often changed addresses without notifying the school. If off campus students were paying their bills and attending classes, there was no reason to question their personal living arrangements, unless the family inquired. When asked if anyone had ever heard of Ways, the Dean of Students gave him one of Father Michael's new brochures. He said a priest had been observed on campus handing them out and posting them on various bulletin boards including in the popular student center.

Detective Talbot also visited the two churches in Oakton with mostly black congregations, as well as several charismatic apostolic churches on the outskirts of town. All of these church pastors knew Father Michael. He had been visiting with their members for more than two years and invited everyone to come to evening services at Ways on Sutter Court. He promised them that life in Ways meant free food and housing, as well as financial support and communal fellowship for life.

At each of these churches, Detective Talbot asked how many of the church members left and joined Ways. In general the common answer was, "Quite a few tried it, but not all stuck with it." The main criticism seemed to be that while it was true about the free food and spiritual fellowship, the free housing was still limited and the financial support was based on all members giving all their money to Father Michael and Ways which would then support all the members' lifelong needs. This arrangement appealed to the needs of the poorest and the weakest who quickly joined. They embraced being told how to live and what to believe. For them, controlled behavior was a joy and comfort. But it was suspicious to others who were more economically and spiritually healthy. They still had dreams and expectations of building better lives for their families and moving ahead in life on their own.

"Even if Father Michael is only fully supporting the members who are living on the property full-time, I can't figure out how he is collecting enough money to stay ahead financially," Detective Talbot confided to Detective Moore. "How can he afford to pay rent and feed and completely support all these people if the majority of Ways members had little or no income to contribute?"

"I think it's fair to assume that Ways living there now are the poorest and the weakest of the total membership. Some of them may receive small government assistance checks and food stamps which they turn over to Father Michael. Others might still be working at low paying jobs for cash which they contribute," Detective Moore suggested. "And didn't Officers Williams and Holmes say Father Michael works construction jobs with that front loader?"

Detective Talbot shook his head. "It still doesn't seem like there would be enough to provide for the crowd of people we saw gathering for the evening services. He must be collecting large sums from pledges from the wealthier members who are still working and living off-site. To me that seems like a risky arrangement. If a member becomes unhappy and drops out of the commune, the payments would stop. I'm betting he's getting money from another source. I think it's time we tried to talk to Martha Sutter. She may be an invalid who's deaf and doesn't speak, but she's still the property owner and Father Michael's landlord. She may know or suspect something unusual is going on. There must be someone here on the force who knows sign language and can help us interview her alone. We want this to be a private meeting without Hope Brown present."

()

Chapter 22

When Father Michael woke up the next morning, he felt stiff and disoriented. He had slept all night on the settee in the sitting room. His mouth was so dry his tongue stuck to the roof of his mouth. He still felt dizzy, but he pulled the blanket around his shoulders and stood up slowly and walked to the kitchen.

Hope was there preparing breakfast for Ways, but when she saw how pale and unsteady he was, she quickly stopped and went to help him. She put her arm around his waist and guided him to a chair at the table. "How do you feel?" she asked.

"Water," he answered hoarsely.

Hope felt his head and then filled a water glass. "You feel feverish. Come upstairs with me and get into bed. I have some aspirin you can take."

After he drank the water, he struggled to his feet and with Hope's help, he climbed the stairs to the second floor. He collapsed on their bed and fell asleep again before she could give him the aspirin. She stood staring at him and then covered him with a quilt. After she left the room she leaned against the closed door. She had been unprepared for the quick debilitating effects of her aunt's poison on Michael. He had always been so strong and in charge and she had loved him. Now she felt worried about the future and at the same time guilty that she was participating in his serious illness.

Downstairs, Walter and a few of Ways were eating breakfast when Hope came in. "We missed Father Michael last night. How's he feeling?" he asked.

Hope shook her head. "He's still not feeling well. I don't know what's wrong with him. Maybe he caught the flu on his trip. If that's what it is, he could be contagious, so everyone should stay away from him. We can't handle a lot of sick people here."

Walter frowned. "So we should probably cancel services, right?"

"Don't do it yet," Hope warned. "Let's see how Michael is when he wakes up again. Telling members not to gather would have to be his decision. He would be furious if you did that on your own."

"All right," Walter grumbled. "Anyway, except for the members who live here, I wouldn't know how to tell the others not to come. Do you have their phone numbers or anything?"

Hope shrugged and poured coffee for herself and Martha. "Michael is the only one who knows the members' personal information. You know how strict he is about secrecy," she said and left the kitchen with the coffee.

Martha was sitting up in bed squeezing bits of Oleander into the small jar. She quickly hid the small container under the covers when Hope came in. "Where's Michael?" she signed.

"Still sick. Now he has a fever," Hope signed back. "Is this what you thought would happen?"

Martha frowned. "I don't know what's going to happen or how long this will take. I just remember my father warned me that even though the Oleander plant is exotic and beautiful, it can be deadly."

"I'm telling Ways Michael has the flu. They'll think he's contagious and they'll have to stay away from him. He won't have a doctor come near him and he would never go to the hospital. So we don't have to worry about anyone from the outside examining him," Hope signed.

Martha nodded. "Good. We'll take care of everything ourselves here."

Martha's grim message made Hope feel nervous and afraid. Before she could answer her, there was a loud knocking on the front door. It frightened her even more and she jumped up, "There's someone here," she franticly signed and hurried out of the room."

"Tell them to go away!" Martha mouthed.

"Good morning, Mrs. Brown" Officer Williams greeted her when she opened the Medusa knocker. "We have a few more questions. May we come in?"

"It's awfully early. We're just having breakfast. Please come back later," she suggested.

Officer Williams cleared his throat. "We're sorry to be disturbing you, but this won't take long and we have a busy day ahead."

Hope couldn't think of another reason to make them go away, so she nervously opened the door. Officers Williams and two men is dark suits and a woman officer walked into the foyer. "Thank you for seeing us. We're actually here to talk to your aunt, Martha Sutter. This is Detective Moore and Detective Talbot. They are going to be taking over the investigation, and this is Officer Jenkins. She knows sign language, so we won't need to take up your time. Would you please tell your aunt we're here?" Officer Williams explained.

"Is this really necessary? She's an old, deaf woman, and she gets confused. She never leaves the house and she doesn't even know the Monroes," Hope complained.

"We know that, but we still need to talk to her. We promise it won't take long. Please Mrs. Brown," he pressed.

Hope felt jittery and sweaty. She didn't know what to do, but she finally pointed to the sitting room, "You can wait in here. I'll see what she says."

Martha was still sitting in bed, pressing Oleander leaves. "Who was that?" she signed.

"Officer Williams from the police is back. He brought two detectives and an officer who knows sign language. They want to talk to you."

Martha held up both of her hands and mouthed, "Why me?"

"Maybe it's about the duplicate keys," Hope signed.

"Bring me one of my black silk robes," Martha angrily motioned. As soon as she was dressed, she had Hope wheel her into the solarium and inside the ferns where she always felt secure and calm.

After Hope did as Martha requested, she showed the officers and detectives into the room. When they entered the solarium, all four stood still, staring in surprise. None of them had seen such an exotic room with so many lush tropical plants and unusual flowers. There was certainly no place like it in Oakton. It took several minutes before they realized Martha Sutter was sitting among the enormous ferns. The fronds framed her face and hugged her body in the wheelchair.

Hope broke the silence and signed and said, "Aunt Martha, this is Officers Williams and I'm sorry I forgot your names," she said turning to the other officer and the detectives.

Officer Jenkins stepped forward and signed her name to Martha and then introduced Detectives Moore and Talbot.

Martha nodded her head and motioned for them to move closer to her. Officer Williams turned to Hope. "We want to speak privately with your aunt. Would you mind waiting in the other room?"

Hope quickly signed to Martha, "They want me to leave. Will you be all right?" Martha nodded and flicked her hand to wave her away. Officer Williams closed the French doors behind Hope and stood in front of them.

"Thank you for seeing us," Detective Moore began the conversation while Officer Jenkins signed.

"What do you want?" Martha asked.

"We're investigating a burglary at your old cottage down the street. It appears someone was able to enter the house by possibly unlocking one of the doors. The current owners of the house have said you and your niece gave them two sets of keys at the real estate closing. Is that correct?"

Martha nodded and held up two fingers.

"And no others exist?" he asked.

"I don't know of any," she answered.

"What about your tenant Michael Brown or one of the other people staying here? Could they have found a duplicate set?" he continued.

Martha frowned. "If they did, how would they know what the keys were for?"

"When did you first meet Michael Brown?"

"Mark Green brought him here. He's my realtor and an old friend."

"So Mark Green closed your rental deal?"

Martha nodded.

"Do you have a copy of the rental contract?" he asked

"Mark keeps it for me."

For most of the interview, Detective Moore had been pacing around the solarium plants while Officer Jenkins stood in front of Martha and signed for him, but now he slowly approached Martha in the ferns and stopped. "Does your contract allow Michael Brown to make changes to your property, operate it as a multi-family complex, and hold nightly meetings with more than one hundred people in your barn?"

This last question took Officer Jenkins several minutes to sign to Martha. When she was finished she turned to Detective Moore, "This is too much for her. Look, she's shaking. We need to stop."

And it was true. Martha's head had rolled to the side with her eyes closed. Her face was pasty white and her body was trembling. She suddenly had become ancient and frail.

Detective Moore took her icy hand and rubbed it between his palms. He looked at Officer Jenkins. "Ask her if she is all right. Does she need a doctor?"

Martha shook her head and mouthed, "Just Hope."

"Tell her we're sorry we upset her and we'll leave now," he said and motioned to Officer Williams to open the doors. Hope rushed in as the officers and detectives quickly left.

Martha opened her eyes, sat up straight and wheeled herself out of the ferns. "Brandy quick!" she signed.

"Are you feeling sick?" Hope asked, as Martha sipped the brandy.

Martha rested her head against the back of the wheelchair. "I'm all right. I didn't like all the questions, so I acted faint. It's easy for an old deaf woman in a wheelchair to fool others!"

Hope laughed. "You looked pretty convincing. What did they want to talk to you about?"

"You were right. They did ask about duplicate keys for the cottage, but mostly they wanted to know about Michael's rental contract and the people he's brought with him. They know about others staying here and the ones who come here every night. They suspect HIM of something. NOT US!" Martha smiled and signed.

Relief flooded over Hope. "So it's Michael and Ways they're after. That's great news. I think I'll go check on him and see how he's doing."

"If he's awake, bring him to me. We'll have some tea together," Martha signed and then patted the inside pocket of her wheelchair.

()

chapter 23

Mark Green was paging through real estate listings in his office. Winter was a slow time for the housing market and he was bored. No one wanted to look at properties or move during the cold months. Hopefully, business would pick up as soon as spring approached. He looked up in surprise when Detectives Moore and Talbot walked in and introduced themselves. He stood up and asked if he could be of help.

"We're investigating a burglary at a house on Sutter Court. Two persons of interest live in the Sutter mansion. One of them is Michael Brown who rents the property, even though the owner Martha Sutter still lives there. She told us you handled the lease arrangement and you are holding her copy of that lease. If that's true, we'd like to take a look at it," Detective Talbot explained.

Mark nodded. "Yes. I had the mansion rental listing for a long time. No one was interested because Martha, who's deaf and only uses sign language, insisted she and her niece Hope would continue to live in parts of the house. Also the house had a number of necessary repair issues which Martha chose to ignore. Michael Brown was different. He wanted to live there and take care of the property. He was willing to go along with the weird living arrangement and the sign language issue."

"Could we see the lease, Mr. Green?" Detective Moore asked.

Mark went to his file cabinets and pulled out a folder. "It's just a standard lease."

The detectives read through the document and agreed it was standard except for the unusual living arrangement. "What about this line about Michael Brown wanting the immediate option to buy the property if or when she wanted to sell?" Detective Talbot asked.

"The option to buy the property is not that unusual in a rental lease. But it's usually the owners who put that in because they are thinking of selling in the future. I thought it was a bit strange for Michael to request it, but Martha didn't seem to mind," Mark explained.

Detective Moore handed back the lease. "Have you been up to the Sutter property since the lease was signed?"

Mark shook his head. "I talked to Hope over the phone after the first year of the lease. She said her aunt wanted to continue renting to Michael for as long as he wanted to stay. It sounded like they had worked out a comfortable living arrangement."

"Did Hope mention that additional people were moving into the property? Or that Michael Brown dresses like a priest, calls himself Father Michael, and has established a community called Ways up there? Did she tell you he's holding large meetings with more than one hundred people in the barn every night?" Detective Moore asked.

Mark was completely confused. "What? A Priest? No! What are you talking about? He wasn't dressed as a priest when he rented the house. He said he was a family counselor and wanted to set up a practice there. The only thing Michael said about extra people was that he had a large family who would help him clean up the property. I assumed a few of them might be staying at the house temporarily. How could he be holding meetings in the barn? It's full of antiques and other personal Sutter belongings."

"Not anymore," Detective Moore said. "It's been modernized. Now it's a meeting house with rows of benches and a pulpit. He's added bathrooms and a small kitchen and the loft has become a dormitory space. The outbuildings have been turned into multi-family homes. Between the barn, the outbuildings and the extra bedrooms in the mansion, there are about twenty or more people living up there full-time. And he has plans to expand and build more units."

Mark sat down in his chair. "Do Martha and Hope know about this?"

Detective Talbot nodded. "Hope certainly knows. She's married to Michael now and helps him with these meetings and with feeding all the extra people."

"We tried to ask Miss Sutter about the situation, but she became very upset and we ended the interview," Detective Moore added. "So it's not clear if she's fully aware of what's going on."

"Are you saying Michael Brown has started some sort of commune on Sutter Court and no one in town has noticed?" Mark asked.

"No one has filed a complaint so far, but one older couple noticed the strange activity. So they bought the house next door from Miss Sutter to protect themselves and keep Michael from taking it over. It's rented to a young University couple now," Officer Williams answered.

"You're talking about that sweet Queen Ann cottage that

old Mr. Sutter built for Martha and her fiancee before the War?" Mark asked.

Detective Moore nodded. "That's the one and it's the same house that had a burglary during Christmas week while the tenants were away."

"Interesting," Mark mused. "The cottage used to be part of the mansion property years ago. It's still the closest house to it. There's probably still a path in back of it that runs through the woods to the barn."

Detective Talbot cocked his head. "So it's possible someone could walk to the back of the cottage on this path?"

"If it's still there and not too overgrown, you could," Mark said.

The detectives closed their notebooks, shook hands with Mark and thanked him for his help. Mark shook his head. "I can't believe any of this. If there's anything else I can do, let me know. I feel terrible that I introduced Michael Brown to the Sutters, and now he's taking advantage of the them. My grandfather was friendly with Mr. Sutter and knew Martha when she was younger. I was in school with Hope. She was very shy and didn't talk much. Everyone knew her parents were deaf and her home life was different. We all just sort of left her alone. And now she's married to Michael and part of a commune. It's unbelievable."

()

Chapter 24

February was just as miserably cold as January. The old cottage furnace was running constantly, but it was a struggle to keep the house warm. Branch and Livy were huddled up with Rory in front of the fireplace. They were happy it was Saturday and no one needed to leave the house. "Have you seen Father Michael?" Livy asked Branch

Branch shook his head. "Not since that day on campus at the beginning of the semester. Maybe he's away again. That front loader has been parked up there on the hill in the same place for weeks."

"I haven't seen Hope either. I wonder if she's all right. She was so upset and strange that last time she was here," Livy worried. "Wonder if she's seen a doctor yet. You know Father Michael doesn't want her to because Ways doesn't believe in outside medical help."

"How far along do you think she is? Branch asked

Livy thought for a minute and looked out the window as a car stopped in front of the house. "I'm only guessing, but maybe six months. Oh Branch! I think the police are here again," she gasped.

Branch opened the front door, just as Officer Williams and the detectives stepped onto the porch. "What's going on? Has something happened?" he asked

Officer Williams introduced the two detectives and explained they were now in charge of the investigation. "They've just learned that there may be an old path leading from the back of your house through the woods to the barn on the Sutter property. We're going back there now to check. Could we go out through your back basement door?"

"Of course," Branch agreed and grabbed his jacket. "I'm coming with you if you don't mind. So do you think maybe whoever was in here used the path to come and go?"

"We'll see what we find," Detective Moore answered.

"Did you find out anything about other keys to this house?" Livy asked.

Detective Talbot shook his head. "Miss Sutter and Mrs. Brown both said they don't know of any other duplicate keys, but of course, it's possible some do exist."

Branch unbolted the basement door and motioned to the men to follow him down the wooden stairs. "I'll be back in a few minutes, Honey. Lock this door behind us and keep the front door locked too."

Livy nervously grabbed Branch's arm. "Why do you have to go with them?"

"I just want to see if they actually find a path. I'll be right back," he promised.

The back yard was mottled with patches of dirty snow and mud. At the end of the lot there was an old metal gate. Ed Baker had wired it shut after the break-in so no one could get in or out. The left side of the yard was bordered by the woods which connected to the Sutter property. The brown underbrush was very thick and revealed no sign of a path. "Let's climb over that gate. It was probably installed sometime later when the path wasn't being used any longer," Officer Williams suggested.

The four men pulled themselves over the rusty gate and dropped into squishy mud on an old, narrow, dirt road that resembled an alleyway going nowhere. Open trash barrels, piles of empty beer bottles and a fire pit were on the other side of the road. "Do you burn your garbage back here?" Officer Williams asked.

Branch shook his head. "Of course not, but they do," he said, pointing to the back of a dilapidated building. "That's some sort of a boarding house."

Officer Williams chuckled. "That's the old Broadway Hotel. We know it well down at the station. It's sort of a hotel-no-tell, if you know what I mean. Mostly down-on-their luck men live there. They spend what money they have on booze, cigarettes and women. We're called there from to time when there's trouble."

"They've never bothered us," Branch said. "But then we don't come back here. All this garbage causes a lot of rat activity. We can see big fat ones feeding from our kitchen window. This is my first time outside that gate," he laughed.

Detective Talbot had walked ahead into the woods where the alley seemed to end. "Come on up this way," he called. "I can see what looks like a trace of a path."

The narrow foot path stretched deep into the thick woods. Dim shadowy sunlight filtered through the trees. After about fifteen minutes of climbing through the overgrown path, the men could see a large dark shape eerily looming up ahead through the trees. The same uneasy feeling from the cemetery scare came over Branch and he stopped walking. "This is taking longer than I expected. I don't want Livy to get worried. I need to go back to the house. Let us know if you find out anything," he said, hurrying away.

The detectives and Officer Williams shrugged to each other and then moved ahead up the path. They stopped in the thick trees in back of the Sutter barn. No human activity was visible from there. Still using the trees as a shield, they edged around toward the front of the structure. From here they could see two figures walking from the house toward the barn. One of them was Father Michael wearing his priest collar tucked under a bathrobe and a jacket. He was leaning heavily on another man who had his arm around him and appeared to be helping him walk. Even from a distance, Officer Williams could see the change in Father Michael's appearance. He looked very pale and weak, and much thinner than the last time he had spoken with him.

"Father Michael Brown is the one in the bathrobe leaning on the other man. Something's happened to him since I last saw him. He looks very sick, like death walking," Officer Williams whispered. "We should set up a visit with him so I can introduce you and we can find out what's wrong with him. If we need another reason we can say it's about the candleholders."

The detectives and Officer Williams crept back to the path and hurried back to the cottage. Both Branch and Livy answered "No" when he asked if they had seen Father Michael lately.

"We just watched him from the woods being helped from the house to the barn. He appears to be very sick and too weak to walk on his own," Officer Williams said.

Branch looked at Livy. "The last time I saw him was early

in January. He was handing out Ways flyers on campus. He seemed fine then."

"A few weeks ago Hope told me Father Michael was away in Boston. I hope he's not seriously ill," Livy added.

"Did she tell you why he went to Boston?" Detective Moore asked.

Livy shook her head. "No, and I don't think she knew."

"So the path really did lead to the barn?" Branch asked.

"It wasn't hard for us to follow, but after dark it would be a different matter," Detective Talbot said. "Someone would have to be very familiar with it. A stranger could easily get disoriented and drift off into those thick woods."

"But whoever ran out of here that night could have used it," Branch emphasized and the detectives and Officer Williams agreed, as they stood up to leave.

"What about the Broadway Hotel people? Couldn't they have just run back over there?" Branch asked.

Officer Williams shook his head. "That's unlikely. Nobody over there is in any condition to run anywhere, but one of us will pay them a visit anyway. And if Father Michael is able to see us, we'll set up a time so I can introduce him to Detectives Moore and Talbot."

()

Chapter 25

With Hope's help, Father Michael continued to have coffee with Martha on most mornings. After a long night's rest, he usually felt stronger, but as the day wore on, his strength evaporated and he found it hard to breathe. By late afternoon he was too weak to sit with Martha for sherry time. If Hope was too busy to help him upstairs to bed, he slipped into a deep sleep in the sitting room.

He was still unable to conduct evening services, recruit new members, or collect earnings from members who worked outside Ways. His lucrative construction jobs were completely out of the question. He had used up most of the large sum of money the Elders had sent him for all the necessary renovations when he first rented the Sutter property. The cold reality was he was quickly running out of money and would soon be unable to operate Ways. Just the day before, Hope had shown him a long list of groceries and supplies she needed to buy to continue feeding and supporting the Ways. He had given her a small amount of the emergency cash he kept on hand, but he knew it wouldn't be enough. Walter and Hope were doing the best they could to keep the commune operating, but with funding and his reserve cash running out, and attendance at nightly services dropping off, the future of

The Way in Oakton was in question.

Father Michael knew he should contact Bishop John and the other Elders on the Ways Planning Board, but he kept putting it off. He dreaded having to ask for more funding which for him meant admitting failure. Over and over he prayed the illness would pass and he'd feel normal again and able to regain control, but with each passing day, his normal seemed farther and farther away. Worst of all he had failed to enact his plan to quietly get rid of Martha Sutter, so he could gain ownership of the property for Ways through Hope's inheritance.

On this particular day, he had walked over to the barn with Walter, but it had proven to be too much for him. Walter had helped him upstairs to bed where he collapsed. Every part of his body felt limp. Hope had come in to sit with him. Even though she despised him for what he was trying to do to her and Aunt Martha, she felt sad about his obvious painful suffering. "Can I get you anything?" she asked quietly.

"I just need to rest. I shouldn't have gone to the barn earlier. I don't understand what's happening to me. I've never been seriously sick in my life," he answered hoarsely.

"Even healthy people like you get sick, Michael. You're just like the rest of us," she smiled. "I don't suppose you want to see a doctor who could help you, do you?"

Father Michael shook his head. "Never," he whispered. "Nature will take its course. That's what we believe. Remember?"

Hope nodded and tucked a quilt around him. "All right then, I'm going out for supplies. Walter is downstairs if you need anything . I won't be gone long." On her way out, she stopped to check on Martha.

"How's Michael?" Martha signed.

Hope frowned. "He's very weak. Did you give him more drops this morning?"

Martha nodded. "He held my hand, but his hand was very limp. His strength is almost gone."

"I know he's an evil man and he wants to harm us, but I can't help feeling sorry for him. His suffering is unbearable. I just want this to be over," Hope signed.

Martha patted her hand . "We have to be strong and finish this. With him gone, all these other people will leave. We'll have our home to ourselves, and you'll have your baby."

Hope nodded and left for her shopping trip. Alone in her little blue Rambler, she leaned back against the seat and closed her eyes. She believed her aunt was right, but she felt the old loneliness of being in the big house alone with her invalid aunt, and now soon she would have a newborn too. She knew nothing about taking care of babies and children. How would she manage alone? Who would help her? She anxiously started the car and sped down the driveway, but she had to slam on the brakes near the bottom when the detectives' black sedan unexpectedly turned into the entrance. The car stopped and Officer Williams jumped out.

"Are you all right, Mrs. Brown?" he asked.

Hope nodded. "I'm sorry. I'm in a hurry to get to the store. I didn't see you turning in. Is there something I can help you with?"

"We need to continue our conversation with your husband. Is he home?" he asked.

"He's home, but he's sleeping. We think he has the flu. I'm

trying to get to the store before he wakes up. You can't talk to him today."

"We'll come back another time. Has he seen a doctor?"

Hope shook her head. "Michael doesn't believe in doctors. I really need to be going. Could you move your car?"

"Of course. We'll come back in a few days," he said and went back to the car.

Hope clinched the steering wheel and waited for them to drive away. "Oh Michael, could you just hurry up and leave us," she whispered. Then she pulled down the street and parked across from Branch and Livy's house.

Livy opened the front door when she saw Hope coming up the walk. "I'm so glad to see you. Branch and I were just talking about how we hadn't seen you and Father Michael in a while. How are you?"

Hope sat down in a chair. "I'm all right, but Michael's sick. We think he has the flu."

"I'm so sorry to hear that. There are a few people at work who have it too. You and your aunt should be careful and try not to catch it. Elderly people can become seriously ill and you're pregnant. How are you feeling?" Livy asked.

"I feel fine. Michael and I are sleeping in separate bedrooms to be safe. But I'm starving all the time and none of my clothes fit. I want to see a doctor. Can you help me find one?"

Livy smiled. "I still have a few maternity clothes you could borrow. I don't have a doctor here in Oakton, but I could ask Rory's pediatrician to recommend an obstetrician. Otherwise, you could probably get a referral from the hospital."

Hope stood up and went to the door. "I knew you could help me. Thank you for being my friend, but don't tell Michael about me seeing a doctor. He and the Ways would forbid it."

"That's ridiculous," Livy snapped. "Decisions about your health and your baby's should be up to you."

"I know, but it's just one of his rules. Please don't tell him," she pleaded.

Livy nodded. "I'll have to find my maternity clothes. Is it all right for me to bring them up to your house?"

"Of course. You and Branch and Rory are always welcome. And you won't forget to ask about a doctor?" Hope asked again.

"I promise I'll ask," Livy assured her and waved good-bye.

When Branch came home from the library, he found Livy and Rory looking through the stacks of unpacked boxes in the basement. "What's going on?" he laughed.

"Hope was here earlier. She asked me to help her find a doctor," Livy said.

"So you're looking through these boxes for one?" he joked.

Livy smirked. "Very funny. I offered to lend her some if my old maternity clothes. They're here somewhere."

"That poor woman doesn't have anything does she?" Branch sighed.

Livy opened another box. "No, she's completely unprepared for this baby. This is the box I was looking for. Could you carry it upstairs?"

"Don't give her anything you really want. I doubt you'll ever see it again," Branch warned.

"I'll be careful," Livy frowned. "I just feel so sorry for her.

She has no one to help her."

Branch put his arms around her. "I know honey, but you can't get too close to that situation up there. A few clothes and a doctor's phone number. That's it. Okay?"

Livy nodded. "Hope said she thinks Michael has the flu. So maybe that's why he looked so weak to Officer Williams and the detectives."

"Just another reason for you to keep your distance from them," Branch grumbled.

chapter 26

A few days later, Livy took the day off work, and sent Rory off to the University Daycare with Branch. She didn't want him to know she was planning to go see Hope. After they left, she packed up the freshly cleaned maternity clothes in a shopping bag along with the name of an obstetrician and walked up the street to the Sutter mansion.

When she reached the house, she noticed a black car parked under the portico. Her first thought was that she should come back another time, but when she saw the Medusa head door knocker, she was fascinated and had to get a closer look. Although it was artistically seductive and captivating, she wondered why anyone would have such a foreboding ornament on their front door. Unless, of course, they were signaling, "Don't Dare To Knock!" As she reached up to touch the entwined silver snakes, the door swung open and she jumped back and lost her balance.

Detective Talbot rushed out and caught her just before she fell backwards down the steps. "Are you hurt, Mrs. Monroe?"

Livy caught her breath. "No, I don't think so. Thank you," she answered shakily. Hope and Detective Moore stepped out and helped her inside. "I was just about to knock when the door suddenly opened and it scared me," she laughed. "I'm really fine, just embarrassed." She turned to Hope. "I brought you a few things."

After the detectives left, Hope took Livy's arm. "Are sure you aren't hurt?" she asked.

Livy smiled and nodded. "To tell you the truth, your unusual door knocker almost scared me away. Is that its purpose?"

"That's my aunt's sadistic sense of humor. Look at this. I can open the eyes from inside to see who's at the door!" she said and demonstrated how the slot opened. "Aunt Martha doesn't like strangers coming here."

"What do all the members of your community think of it?" Livy asked.

"They don't come in through the front door. If they come to the house for food, they use the kitchen door. The ones who sleep upstairs go in and out that way too. I doubt they've even noticed Medusa. Come have a cup of tea with me," Hope offered and led her into the dining room.

Livy slipped off her coat and sat down at the big table with the silver candlesticks. "I guess you know what Medusa represents in mythology," she said while Hope poured the tea.

Hope shook her head. "Not really, but I'm sure Aunt Martha knows. You tell me."

Livy laughed. "All right, but it's just a story. Here's what I remember. In Greek mythology, Medusa, who was a mortal human, and her two immortal sisters were monsters called Gorgons. The lived on an island called The Terrible Sisters Island. They were known for their deadly powers and everyone was afraid of them. They had wings and live twisting snakes for hair-just like your door knocker. If a human looked into a Gorgon's eyes, he or she would immediately be turned to stone. With the help of some of the Greek gods and their magical powers, a brave young man was able to kill Medusa, cut off her head and escape with it in a bag while the other sisters were sleeping. Strangely, the evil head kept its killing power and it had to be kept hidden away forever, so no one would risk looking at it."

Hope shook her head. "Huh, imagine having the power to turn someone to stone with just a look. How do you know all this, Livy? It's so gruesome."

"I studied ancient history and mythology in college. Some stories just stick in your head," she smiled and opened the shopping bag. She handed Hope the paper with the doctor's information and took out the clothes.

Hope slipped the paper in her pocket and looked through the clothes. "Thank you. I think these will fit."

"What's all this?" Father Michael asked, shuffling into the room.

Hope's face turned red. "I thought you were sleeping. Are you feeling better?"

He slumped into a chair at the far end of the table. "Could you get me some water?"

"Livy is loaning me some maternity clothes," she answered nervously and hurried to get the water.

Father Michael stared at Livy. "That's nice of you, but you should leave before you catch what I have. I wouldn't have come down, if I had known you were here," he said hoarsely.

Shocked by his changed appearance and frail condition,

Livy quickly put on her coat. "I should be going anyway. I have to pick up Rory soon," she lied. "Take care of yourself, Michael."

Hope came out of the kitchen and handed him his water. Livy hurried to the door, but not before she noticed that he had to hold the glass with two hands, because he was shaking so badly. Hope followed Livy to the door and thanked her again.

"I'm happy to help. I didn't get a chance to ask you, but are the police or those two detectives still bothering you about our break in? Is that why they were here?" Livy asked.

"They seem to think one of our members might have done it, but I couldn't help them much with that," she answered in a low voice.

Livy frowned. "Do you believe that?"

Hope opened the door and patted Livy on the back. "I don't know what I believe. My world is so upside down right now. I don't know what's going to happen," she answered and then gave a strained laugh. "Remember, Don't Look Back At Medusa when you leave! I don't want you to turn to stone."

After Livy left, Hope went back and sat down with Michael. "Detectives Moore and Talbot were here earlier. They're in charge of the Monroe break in now. They wanted to talk to you, but I told them you were too sick to see them."

He leaned his head against the back of the chair and closed his eyes. "What did they want this time?"

"They brought over the two silver candleholders the police found at Branch and Livy's after the break in. They wanted to see if they matched the ones here on the table," Hope sighed.

"And of course they did. What did you say?" he mumbled.

"I told them there are lots of silver candleholders like these throughout the house. They've been here for many years, way before electricity was added. We probably wouldn't notice if any were missing."

"Good answer Hope," he whispered. "But it's clear they suspect someone from here, maybe us, left them at the Monroes'."

Tears rolled down Hope's cheeks. "I don't want to talk to any of them anymore," she sniffed.

"Then don't. Let them think whatever they want. Maybe it's one of our Ways who come here for evening services or maybe it's someone else. They don't have any proof, and you don't need to tell them anything else about our community," Michael insisted. "What's your aunt doing? I missed having coffee with her this morning. See if I can sit with her now, before the weakness gets worse."

Hope was relieved to get away from Michael's angry frustration. She found Martha paging through one of her botanical books in the solarium. "Michael is awake. He wants to have coffee with you now," she signed.

Martha looked over her glasses and smiled. "Good. Bring the coffee to me first before he comes in," she signed.

Hope went back for Michael, but he had fallen asleep and she had to shake him awake. He stared at her blankly when she told him Martha was fixing herself up a little for him. "I'll take the coffee in first and come back to help you. Do you understand?" He nodded and watched her prepare the coffee tray and take it to the solarium.

"All set?" she signed to Martha after she set the tray down on her table.

"Yes," Martha whispered as she poured two drops from her little jar into Michael's cup and placed it on his chair next to hers.

"I'll help him in here. He's very tired. He may fall asleep on you," Hope signed.

Father Michael shuffled to the solarium with Hope holding onto him. Because his breathing was so labored, he had to stop every few steps to lean on the furniture or against the doors so he could catch his breath. She helped him to the chair next to Martha and handed him his coffee. He took a few sips and managed a faint smile at Martha while Hope left the room. Martha studied him closely and picked up her chalk board. "You look terrible," she wrote. Michael glumly nodded his head, but he didn't write an answer.

"Doctor?" she wrote.

"NO!" he whispered and sipped more of his coffee.

"What can I do to help you?" Martha scribbled.

Michael picked up his chalkboard and slowly wrote, "I can't pay my rent or the utility bills"

"Don't worry. Delay the rent until you feel better. I'll pay all the utilities," she printed.

"Thank you," he whispered and took her hand. The two of them sat peacefully together, drinking their coffee until he fell asleep and his cup slipped to the floor, but Father Michael didn't notice the clatter. Although his eyes were closed, his thin, withering hand stayed entwined in her boney, wrinkled fingers.

Martha watched him and smiled. "It's almost over my dear. This time it's me letting you go and saying good-bye my way and forever. Revenge is wonderfully sweet after all these years," she whispered.

()

Chapter 27

To Martha and Hope's surprise and disappointment, Michael was still alive in the spring. He had a gaunt, ghost-like appearance, and he was now too weak to leave the upstairs, but he hung onto life even as it slowly ebbed away. He depended on Hope to help him to the bathroom and bring him his meals, although he ate very little. She had taken over giving him the Oleander drops, because he was unable to sit with Martha. He was only awake for a few hours a day, and then he often slept so deeply that Hope was unable to wake him up. Each time she checked on him, she expected him to be dead.

At the same time, Walter had begun turning Ways away from the evening services and suggesting to the members living on the property they should begin looking for other arrangements. When Father Michael learned about what he was doing, he became very angry and demanded Walter explain himself.

Nervously, Walter pointed out there was no one qualified to lead Ways or conduct the nightly services. Many of the members who still worked had become belligerent and refused to make their monthly payments. Some were demanding to be reimbursed the money they had already paid into Ways. Others who didn't work on the outside accepted the declining situation and remained completely dependent on the commune. All of Father Michael's expansion projects had stopped, so there was no construction work to keep them busy. Instead they filled their days and nights with meditation, free food, naps, and frequent sexual relations. At the same time, Hope was being forced to cut back on the food service because there simply wasn't enough to feed everyone.

"Father Michael, **You** are Ways for everyone. Without **You** inspiring us daily about the value of communal living, free love and self-actualization, we are lost. **You** are the reason we're here. I'm sorry, but Ways isn't sustainable without **You**," Walter pleaded.

"You could do it Walter. I can introduce you to the Elders of Ways. We're a much larger organization than you know. They will help you become one of our apostles," Father Michael murmured.

Walter shook his head. "I could never be you. Even as weak as you are right now, you're still stronger than I am. I'm a follower, not a leader. That's why Ways has been so comforting for me. I can be myself here and enjoy being part of a community of equals. No one cares that I'm not a leader. I'll be lost again if I leave."

Father Michael pushed himself up to a sitting position. "I hope you won't leave us, but you must promise to stop interfering with our Ways community and telling people not to come here. Help me to my office. I need to make a call."

Walter left Father Michael hunched over his desk and went downstairs to find Hope. "How did that go?" she asked.

"It didn't go well. I tried to explain to him what's happening with Ways, but he didn't accept it. He's at his desk now. I think he's calling the Elders for help," he mumbled.

Hope shook her head. "He should have done that weeks ago when he first got sick. Now it's probably too late. I feel bad for everyone here who depends on him—on us. What will happen to them now?"

Walter looked down. "He's not going to get better is he? He's like a skeleton. I could feel his bones sticking out when I helped him walk to the office."

"I don't know. I can't believe he wants to die, but he has chosen to let nature take its course. He won't let anyone help him, and now here we are. I don't want him to keep suffering. If he's going to die, I hope it's soon," she sighed.

Walter put his arm around her. "I'm planning to leave the commune soon. It's all going to end without Father Michael. I feel terrible about leaving you here alone. What will you do?"

Hope turned and hugged him. "You're a good man Walter. You're the only one here I can depend on. Please don't go yet. Promise me you'll stay until after this baby is born."

Walter pulled away. "I'll think about it, but when do you think the baby will come?"

Hope smiled. "It's just a few more weeks. Please stay."

"If I stay, I don't want to have anything to do with the birth. I still have nightmares about burying poor Mary and her baby. I will never do that again," he warned.

"You don't have to worry about that. Don't tell Michael, but I'm seeing a doctor and I'm having this baby in the hospital. The most you would need to do is drive me there," Hope whispered.

Walter shrugged. "I don't know. Maybe I'll stay," he offered and hurried out the back door.

Hope went upstairs and stood outside Father Michael's office. She strained to hear him hoarsely talking on the phone. Before he hung up, she thought she heard him say, "You need to come now. I'm not getting better."

She opened the door and put her hand on his shoulder. "Are you all right?" she asked.

He put his ice cold hand over hers. "I've asked the Elders to come down from Boston to take over for me. I don't have the strength to run Ways anymore. I think I'm dying."

Knowing that she and Martha were causing his slow death, she still cried, "Don't say that. You could be better tomorrow!"

But Father Michael shook his head. "My organs are failing. I can't last much longer. You need to accept it and prepare yourself. When the Elders come, you must do what they say. You understand? They'll help you and all the Ways move to one of our other commune settlements. You must do that so our child can grow up and thrive in Ways. My life and work will continue through him or her."

"Oh Michael, I can't leave here. This is my home. Without you, Aunt Martha is my only family," Hope sobbed.

"Don't be an idiot Hope. The Ways are your family. Martha is just a crazy old woman who'll be dead soon too. When you inherit her wealth, you will give it to Ways just as planned," he rasped.

Hope pulled her hand away from his. That's your plan, not mine, she wanted to scream, but instead she willed herself to stay calm. "You've always known what was best for me. I'll do what I can to help the Elders. When are they coming?"

"In a few days," he whispered. "Could you help me back to bed? I'm freezing."

"Of course, just lean on me," she said, as she helped him to stand and walk back to the bedroom. "I'll be right back with some hot tea. That should warm you up." And hopefully that will do it, she said to herself.

()

chapter 28

Branch was furious when Livy told him she had been up to the Sutter house. "What if something had happened to you!" he yelled.

"Nothing happened to me. I'm sorry I didn't tell you, but I knew you wouldn't want me to go. Don't be mad at me." Livy apologized.

Branch stared out the kitchen window to control his temper and finally asked, "What was the house like?"

Livy described the soaring foyer and chandelier and the beautiful rooms she saw. "It's filled with antiques and silver pieces everywhere. And get this. They have a Medusa door knocker on the front door. It has one of those sliding panels behind the eyes so they can see who's standing outside!"

"You're kidding. You have to admit that's just too weird," he laughed.

"Hope says it was Martha Sutter's idea to keep people away. Anyway, it didn't scare me away. Those two detectives were just leaving when I got there. So I don't think her idea is working."

"Why were they there?" Branch asked.

"Hope didn't seem to want to talk about it. All she said was the police and the detectives think maybe some of Ways members could have been responsible for breaking into our house."

"Did you see Father Michael?" Branch asked

"He came downstairs soon after I got there. He's very weak and sick. And he looks completely different. I don't think he's contagious, but he wanted me to leave. You should go see him. I know you like him."

Branch shook his head. "He's an interesting guy. I'm sorry he's sick, but I don't think of him as a friend. And I don't like this whole commune philosophy."

"I don't like any of it either. Maybe I'm wrong, but there don't seem to be as many people going up there at night. Have you noticed?"

"Ed Baker thinks Ways may be losing its appeal. He's hoping they'll pack up and leave the neighborhood for good," Branch answered.

"I wonder what Hope will do, if Father Michael decides to leave," Livy worried. "I'm pretty sure she won't leave her aunt, but then he is her husband, and they'll have a baby very soon."

"Maybe they're not legally married. Father Michael could have just performed some sort of fringe Ways ceremony and said they were man and wife," Branch guessed.

Livy gasped. "You really think he convinced her they were legally married and she believed him?"

Branch sighed. "Remember the saying, 'Love turns a blind eye.' I imagine she believed him at the time, but maybe not now. If they're not legally married, then she has a reason for not leaving here with him. But the baby might be a problem. He may want his child to stay with him in Ways wherever it goes."

"How awful for Hope. She would have to choose between leaving with her husband and baby, or refusing to leave, keeping the baby and staying with her aunt. If she chooses to stay here, then she'll constantly be worrying that Father Michael and Ways might take her baby away at some point. I can't imagine it," Livy moaned.

Branch put his arm around her. "We're outsiders, remember? This isn't our problem. We only see brief glimpses of life at the Sutter mansion. Maybe nothing will change for them at all. And anyway, we're leaving here in a couple of months. And I promise we will never live next to a commune again," he smiled.

"Thank God!" she laughed. "This glimpse has been enough for a lifetime!"

()

chapter 29

Two days later, Bishop John and Brother Paul arrived in Oakton. Before going to Sutter Court, they drove through the charming, small town and walked around the lively University campus. They both agreed that Father Michael had made an excellent choice for a branch of Ways. So why was the settlement in danger of failing, they wondered.

Walter was outside trying to start Father Michael's front loader when the Ways Elders arrived. He jumped out of the cab and walked over to the car as the two men, dressed in the same black priest attire, were getting out. "Can I help you?" he asked.

Bishop John introduced himself and Brother Paul. "We're part of the Ways organization in Boston. Father Michael called us and asked us to come down. Is he here?"

"Welcome to Oakton Ways," Walter smiled. Father Michael said you might be coming. He's sleeping right now. Hopefully, he'll be able to talk to you when he wakes up. Would you like me to show you around while you wait?"

"How is he?" Bishop John asked.

Walter looked down. "He's very sick," he said quietly.

"What about his wife Hope? Is she here?" Brother Paul asked.

Walter shook his head. "She's out doing a few errands, but she should be back soon."

"Let's look around then," Bishop John said. "Thank you for offering to give us a tour."

"Let's start with the barn and the outbuildings." Walter suggested. "Father Michael did an amazing job transforming the barn into the gathering center and there's a dormitory space there too. The outbuildings are living spaces for couples with children."

The atmosphere in the softly lit barn was warm and welcoming. The sound of folk music playing and the smell of coffee permeated the air. A few Ways were sitting on the benches meditating or reading. Several of the women were mending clothes while a small group of toddlers were playing with building blocks and cars and trucks. A team of men were working on plans for expanding the outbuildings into additional living quarters.

Bishop John was very pleased as he stood at the lectern and gazed out at the rows of benches and peaceful Ways. "Just as it should be," he commented quietly to Brother Paul. "He's done a great job here."

Brother Paul agreed and asked Walter to show them the upstairs. The dormitory space in the converted hay loft was clean, but felt cramped and less appealing. Despite the late morning hour, several men were still sleeping on cots. "Why aren't they up and working?" he asked.

"These men are our newest members. They're still adjusting to life here, away from their troubled pasts," Walter explained. "When the weather warms up, we will have them working construction on the expansion of the outbuildings. Let's take a look at those existing buildings now."

"We can only house small families in these two buildings. That's why the expansion project is critical to the commune," he emphasized, as he opened the door to one of the two story structures. "Our plan is to bump out the back walls on both floors and build out into the woods behind. There's at least a half acre there before we hit the road below."

"How many rooms will you gain?" Brother Paul asked.

"We think twenty communal family sleeping rooms, plus bathrooms and showers in each house."

"That sounds ideal. Father Michael's vision for the future here is well thought out and impressive," Bishop John smiled.

Walter nodded. "He's a great leader in every way, but what if he doesn't recover from this sickness? We don't know what will happen."

Bishop John frowned. "Don't worry, my son. We will take care of you. Ways has many other apostles and communal sites like this one. We would send a new apostle here to take over for Father Michael and continue our work. If that didn't work out for some reason, we would move all Oakton members to one of our other locations, if they are willing to go. Here's my card. You can call me anytime, day or night, if you need help. Could we see if Father Michael is awake? We need to talk to him."

Walter stared at the card , but said nothing as he led them around to the back of the mansion. "We use this entrance in the morning for breakfast."

Brother Paul stopped walking and pointed to the field of overgrown weeds and stones. "Is that a cemetery?" he asked.

"Father Michael never mentioned that being part of the property."

"That's the Sutter family cemetery. We've offered to clean it up, but Miss Sutter doesn't want us in there. Some of those graves date back to before the Civil War. It's a shame no one is taking care of it," Walter explained.

Brother Paul stared at him. "But you've been in there haven't you, if you know about the dates on the headstones."

Embarrassed, Walter hung his head. "I like history and I was curious. I just wanted to look around. That's all. And then one other time, a neighbor's little girl got lost in there. Some of us went in to look for her," he said, climbing the steps to the kitchen door.

Hope was unloading groceries when the three men came in. She stepped back when she saw the two strangers, dressed like priests. Walter reached out and steadied her. "It's okay Hope. These men are Father Michael's friends from Ways in Boston. Remember he asked them to come."

Bishop John smiled and introduced himself and Brother Paul. "We're very happy to meet you, Hope. Father Michael has spoken to us about you and your aunt. Congratulations on the baby and bringing us a new Ways member."

Hope managed a small smile. "Have you seen Michael?"

"No, he was sleeping when we got here. Walter was kind enough to show us around the barn and the outbuildings. You and Father Michael are doing great work here, and the plans for expansion are impressive," Bishop John praised.

Hope shrugged. "That was all Michael's doing before he got sick. I just cook, clean and take care of my aunt."

"We'd like to meet your aunt after we talk to Father Michael.

He has spoken very highly of both of you," he continued.

"She doesn't see strangers. She's deaf and doesn't speak. We only talk through sign language."

"But she talks to Father Michael doesn't she?" Brother Paul interrupted.

Hope raised her eyebrows. "Their friendship is unusual. They sit together and enjoy coffee or tea. Sometimes they hold hands or write notes to each other on chalkboards. That's how they talk."

"We'd still like to meet her," Bishop John repeated. "Would you see if Father Michael could see us now?"

"You gentlemen can wait in the dining room. Help yourselves to coffee or tea. If Michael is awake, he'll need a few minutes to get ready for your visit," she said, on her way upstairs.

Walter had stood by quietly during this conversation, but after the Elders settled themselves in the dining room, he excused himself and went back outside to the front loader. He couldn't wait to get away from the obsequiousness of the Elders and all their questions. Hope's obvious dislike of their presence was confusing and unlike her. He had expected her to be reassured that Father Michael had asked them for help, and they had responded so quickly. What was she afraid of and why?

Alone in the dining room, Bishop John and Brother Paul talked about Walter. "He seems like a good Ways member. We should try to convince him to train as an apostle," Bishop John said. "God knows we need more Ways leaders. Eventually, he could take over here."

Brother Paul pursed his lips and pressed his hands together.

"He seems very kind and trustworthy, but he doesn't impress me as a strong leader. He's comfortable assisting Father Michael, but he lacks charisma. I can't imagine him recruiting new members and convincing them Ways is their life now and forever after."

"You surprise me Brother Paul. I remember when you first came to Ways. You were homeless, penniless and addicted to drugs. You had nothing to offer us, but we took you in and you thrived in our free thinking, free love commune. You had all the food, shelter, and brothers and sisters surrounding you. You became strong and one of us, and we shaped you into one of our leaders," Bishop John reminded him.

Hope stood in the doorway listening to these words. Her heart ached for Walter. She had to warn him. She didn't want him to become a strict enforcer like Michael. She needed him to help protect her and the baby and Aunt Martha from Ways after Michael was gone. She cleared her throat and stepped into the dining room. "Michael wants you to come upstairs. He's very weak so you won't be able to stay long."

The Elders stood up without saying a word and followed her up the curved staircase to the bedroom. Father Michael's shrunken body was propped up in the bed. His eyes were closed and sunken back into his translucent gray face. His thick dark hair had thinned to dirty white strings across his scalp. His labored breathing came out in a wheezing sound. "My God! What happened to this good man?" Bishop John asked. "He's a shadow of the young, vibrant Father Michael we know."

"We don't know, but he's never been the same since he came back from Boston," Hope answered quietly.

Father Michael opened his eyes and raised his hand to the men. "Leave us Hope. I need to talk to them alone."

"I'll bring you some tea," she answered and left the room.

Bishop John and Brother Paul pulled chairs up to the bed and leaned in closely so they could hear his whispered words.

"We had no idea you were so sick. What can we do?" Brother Paul asked.

"Thank you for coming," he rasped. "Nothing to do for me. It's too late. I've already begun my journey to the Greater Ways we've all talked about. I see glimpses of it when my eyes are closed. Others I recognize are waiting there for me, for all of us. You'll have to take over here."

Bishop John took Michael's hands and Brother Paul laid his hands on top of theirs as they prayed together. "We'll take care of everything for you. Be strong Father Michael until we see you again," Bishop John finished, just as Hope came in with the tea. "We'll wait for you downstairs," he said solemnly.

She sat down on the bed and held the cup to Michael's lips. "Try to drink a little. It will make you feel better," she pleaded.

"Can't," he whispered.

Hope forced the cup between his lips. "You have to try."

"Burns my throat," he choked, after swallowing.

"Believe me Michael. It's going to help you," she coaxed him again, but he had already slipped into a deep sleep and the tea trickled down his chin. She gently wiped his face before leaving the room and going back downstairs.

"We didn't realize how seriously ill Father Michael is," Bishop John said to Hope when she came in. "If he doesn't recover, you don't need to worry about the future. Ways will take care of your every need forever. Our flight back to Boston leaves soon, but now that we know Father Michael's condition, we have to speak to your aunt before we leave," Bishop John demanded.

Hope agreed to ask, but warned him again that Martha Sutter did not like to see strangers. This time however, Martha surprised her. She said yes to meeting with the Ways Elders and quickly rolled her wheelchair deep into the giant ferns.

Hope motioned to the Elders to follow her. "She will see you for a few minutes in her solarium, but I'll have to stay with you to interpret the sign language."

Martha and Hope both smiled to themselves at the reaction of The Elders when they entered the lush garden. Just like the others who encountered it for the first time, they were hypnotized by all the exotic blooming plants and trees and the heavy scents of gardenias and lilies. Several minutes passed before they realized Martha was sitting amidst the ferns as if they were part of her.

"Hello Miss Sutter," Bishop John managed to say. "Thank you for seeing us."

"This is Bishop John and Brother Paul. They are Michael's friends from the Boston Ways," Hope signed and said.

Martha nodded to them and signed back with her glittering, diamond ringed fingers, "What do you want?"

"Tell her we're here because we're concerned about Father Michael," Brother Paul said.

"We think he's dying," Bishop John added.

Martha nodded. "I will miss him."

"We're concerned about what will happen to his rental

contract with you if he dies," Bishop John said and looked at Hope. "We believe Father Michael wants it to pass to his wife, your niece, so the Ways community will continue on here as your tenant."

Tears flowed down Hope's face as she signed his words, and Martha's reaction was swift. She wheeled her chair out of the ferns and angrily signed and mouthed, "NO! All this ends when Michael dies. He is my tenant, but he stole from me and took advantage of both Hope and me with all this Ways business. Your people will have to move off this property immediately or we will contact the police. This meeting is over. Get out!" she signed and flicked her hand. After she interpreted her aunt's strong words, Hope quickly showed the shocked men out of the solarium and opened the front door.

"We are completely confused by what your aunt said. Do you agree with what she believes? What is she talking about Father Michael stealing from her?" Bishop John asked.

Hope wiped her eyes and tried to answer calmly. "This is her home. She rented parts of it to Michael and no one else. He never mentioned his plan to alter our property and start a commune here. She trusted him, but instead he sold many of the family antiques she had stored in the barn and he used the money for the commune. He took advantage of her because she is old and disabled. And now I know he never loved me. He married me because he thought I would inherit the property someday, and then it would be his too because I am his wife. Even if there's a miracle and he recovers, the trust is broken. No matter what happens to him, one way or another, he and the commune have to leave."

Brother Paul shook his head. "This is an incredibly sad

situation. I think you are wrong about Father Michael's motives and intentions with you. But putting that aside, you and your aunt must understand it will take some time for us to move our members out of here."

"Let's hope it doesn't come to that," Bishop John said, handing her his card. "If Father Michael dies, you must call us right away, and we'll take care of him. We'll also begin contacting our other Ways communities to arrange moving the Oakton members to other locations. You, of course, must come with us too. Father Michael wants you and the baby to be lifelong Ways members. We'll care for you for the rest of your life. It's your destiny and salvation."

Hope said nothing and stood rigidly when both men hugged her briefly and went out the door. Outside they stood on the porch. "Look at that," Brother Paul said, pointing at the Medusa door knocker. Did you notice that when we drove up?"

Bishop John stared at the mythical head. "Martha Sutter is a strange, maybe even evil, woman. Father Michael thought he could manipulate her and her niece to secure this property. He even talked about the possibility of poisoning her, remember?"

"Well, I guess he never got around to that. She doesn't seem sick to me. Unhinged and old yes, but dying no," Brother Paul smirked.

Bishop John agreed. "Despite being elderly and disabled, she turned out to be stronger than Father Michael." The two men stood by their car looking around at the stately Sutter property. "It's too bad this site didn't work out for Ways. It was a perfect choice. I'm afraid Father Michael will be gone soon. We need to start working on the member relocation right away."

()

chapter 30

Early the next morning, Hope checked on Michael. He was very still and cold to the touch. She put her ear to his chest, but could not hear his heart beating. She held his wrist, felt no pulse and then sat back and stared at him. Strange mixed feelings of relief, guilt and sadness flooded over her all at the same time. Michael was gone for good. The ordeal was over. She and her baby and Aunt Martha would be safe. The Sutter property would never belong to Ways. Time seemed to stop for her. Thoughts of what to do next swirled through her head, but she felt completely exhausted and unable to move. Finally, she stood up and pulled the quilt over him, but didn't cover his face. To her, he looked peaceful and calm, almost smiling. "Good-bye Michael, wherever you are," she whispered and left the room.

Walter was downstairs in the kitchen. "I went ahead and started the coffee and the breakfast for the others," he said when Hope walked in. I thought maybe you and Father Michael were sleeping in."

She sat down in the dining room and Walter poured her a coffee. "Michael is dead," she said, gripping the warm cup.

Walter stared at her. "Are you sure? Maybe he's just in one

of those deep sleeps."

"I'm certain. He must have died in his sleep. Go up and see for yourself."

Without saying another word, Walter turned and went upstairs. Just as Hope had described, he found Father Michael's lifeless body. "Oh God, Father, why couldn't you have hung on for all of us. Now we will have to leave," he murmured.

Hope was still sitting in the same chair when he came back down. Other Ways were eating breakfast, so Walter quietly sat down next to her and nodded his head. Neither of them spoke until the others had finished eating and left. "What should we do now?" he asked.

Hope took a deep breath. "I'll call Bishop John. He'll send some Elders to close down the commune and move members to other locations."

"I meant what do we do with Father Michael? We can't just leave him up there on the bed," Walter said, his voice shaking.

"I'll ask them to take him back to Boston and bury him there. It's too dangerous to use the cemetery here. Some of the members might tell outsiders."

Walter thought for a minute. "I suppose you are right, but we should at least hold a special evening service for him here. Everyone loved him. They will be lost without him. At the very least, they should be able to say good-bye and pray for him in the afterlife."

Hope shook her head. "I don't think we should tell anyone he's dead. Let's just say the Elders are coming to take him back to Boston for treatment. We'll leave it to them to explain about the move to another Ways commune. You know I won't leave here

Walter, and you know I want you to stay here too." She stood up and began fixing a breakfast tray for Martha. "Now I have to tell my aunt about Michael. She loved him too in her own way."

Walter watched her walking to the library. He still couldn't believe Father Michael was dead. He felt like running away now. Why should he wait for those Boston Elders to come and upset everyone about moving away? Without Father Michael, he felt alone and abandoned like he was before joining Ways. He was certain it would be the same or worse for the others. He had planned to help Hope and the baby, but now he had to think of himself. The Ways allegiance was gone, and he had to get away. She would have to ask someone else for help.

He climbed the stairs to his small bedroom and shoved his few belongings into a knapsack. He stopped in Father Michael's office to search for the Ways cashbox. Contributions had been dwindling while Father Michael was sick, but a few thousand dollars was still in the box. He figured Ways owed him at least that much for all the extra work he had done for the commune. It was just enough for a bus ticket and a start somewhere else.

While he was pocketing the cash, he heard footsteps in the hallway. Thinking it was Hope, he quickly put the cashbox back in the drawer, shouldered his knapsack, and poked his head out the office door. She wasn't there, so he nervously looked around the upstairs. He was certain he had heard someone walking, but he couldn't find anyone. Sweat soaked his shirt and he felt afraid and trapped. What if Father Michael wasn't dead after all and had seen him take the money? What if he was waiting for him at the bottom of the stairs? With clammy hands, he cracked open the door to the master bedroom and breathed a sigh of relief. Father Michael's body looked exactly the same. In fact he was smiling! Walter turned and ran down the stairs and out the front door. Only the Medusa saw him running down the driveway without looking back.

()

chapter 31

"Thank God that's over. Are you sure he's dead?" Martha signed when Hope told her about Michael.

"Yes. It's strange, but he actually looks like he's smiling," she signed back.

Martha silently laughed. "Good for him. You're going to bury him in the cemetery?"

Hope shook her head. "No. I'm worried one of the Ways might tell someone on the outside that we buried him ourselves. I'll ask the Boston men you met to take his body back there or somewhere. He can't stay here."

Martha sniffed. "He's your husband, not mine. Do what you want and good riddance. Do you have any of the Oleander left?"

"Just a tiny bit. I'll flush it down the toilet. Do you have any?"

Martha handed her the small jar she kept hidden. "That's all of it. How soon will the others be leaving?"

"Don't know," Hope signed. "It will take some time to clear them out and convince others not to come here anymore."

Martha leaned her head back against the pillows. "I blame myself for all of this. I should never have let Michael into my heart. He tried to take everything from me, including you. And now I've done the unforgiveable. I've taken his life. Take this tray away. I don't feel like eating," she signed.

Hope looked at the untouched food. "You should stay in bed and rest today, Aunt Martha. This has all been a terrible strain. I'll come back later with a light lunch. Maybe you'll feel better by then."

Bishop John was not surprised when Hope called. "This is an unbearable loss for all of us," he said. "Someone will be there by tonight to help you. Father Michael will be taken away immediately and we'll take care of everything. Have you told anyone else?"

"Just Walter and Aunt Martha know," she whispered.

"Don't tell anyone else. Just say we're taking him to Boston for treatment. Do you understand?" he asked.

"Yes. Thank you," she managed to say before hanging up.

As soon as the call was over, she went to the barn to find Walter. The commune members were there just like any other day. Music was playing softly while the men and women were working on projects and the children were playing games and looking at books. Several people asked about Father Michael, and Hope repeated that he was still very sick and the Elders were coming to take him away for treatment. No one had seen Walter since the early breakfast.

Hope hurried back to the house to check his room. The door was wide open and none of his belongings were there. She sat down on the bed to think. She knew Walter was afraid to be part of Ways without Michael, but she didn't believe he would run away. She thought she could depend on him. Now no one was going to help her. The enormity of being in charge of what was left of the Sutter family was numbing. She curled up and closed her eyes until the sound of the phone ringing in Michael's office jarred her awake. When she answered, a woman's voice asked to speak to Michael Brown. Half awake and confused, she mumbled, "He can't come to the phone. This is his wife. Can I take a message?"

"This is Amy Tate. I'm a supervisor for the Oakton Social Services Department. We've had an inquiry about families living there with young school aged children who are not enrolled in school. I am calling ahead to let you know we will be coming by to assess the situation."

Hope's hands were shaking."This isn't a good time," she blurted out and hung up. "Dear God what if they come while the men are here taking Michael away!" she whispered and quickly called Bishop John again.

"Try to stay calm Hope," the Bishop soothed. "Two apostles from one of our Kentucky settlements are on their way now. They should be there in less than an hour with a van equipped to transport Father Michael."

Hope's voice was strained. "What if these social workers show up first?"

"Take them to visit the families in the barn or the out-buildings. Try to impress them with how good life is in Ways. You can do this, Hope. Everything will be all right," he reassured her, but she hung up without answering. She needed to tell Martha what was happening.

Hurriedly she prepared a lunch tray and carried it to her. Martha had gotten herself dressed and was waiting in the solarium. "You look terrible," Martha signed when Hope came in. "You haven't even gotten dressed!"

Embarrassed, Hope looked down at her wrinkled chenille robe. "I haven't had time. I'll change now. Some men will be here soon to pick up Michael."

"Good," Martha answered and waved her away.

As she passed the front door, she peaked outside. Sutter Court was quiet, except for a gray van driving up the street. She watched it stop at the bottom of the driveway and then slowly pull up and park at the front steps under the portico. Two large muscular men, dressed in black priest attire, climbed out and opened the back of the van. They pulled out a stretcher and a blanket before going to the door and pulling the Medusa knocker.

Hope leaned against the door for support and forced herself to breathe. Her head was spinning and she had jelly legs, but after taking a few deep breaths, she was able to open the door. The men came in and she took them up the stairs to Michael. She stood by quietly as the men quickly placed him on the stretcher and covered him with the blanket up to his neck. He still looked like he was sleeping and his expression was calm and peaceful.

Hope put her hand over her mouth and watched them carry him down the stairs and load him into the van. After they closed the back door, they silently turned and nodded and then drove away. No one except Hope and the Medusa saw the van glide down Sutter Court and out of sight. Father Michael Brown was gone from her life forever, but she knew their unborn child would be his constant reminder to her of what she had done. Would he or she be like him she wondered? And how many other children had he fathered in Ways? Would they be like him too?

Back inside, she went upstairs and filled trash bags with all the linens Michael had touched. The deeply stained mattress would have to go too, but she left his clothes and personal items in the closet. In case anyone asked, she wanted it to look like he would be coming back after he recovered. Even though it was a chilly spring afternoon, she opened all the windows in the upstairs to let in the fresh air. Then she locked herself in her bathroom, ran a hot bath and tried to scrub away her dark memories.

()

chapter 32

The next day Bishop John along with Brother Paul and Brother Phillip arrived. They went straight to the barn, introduced themselves to the Ways gathered there, and announced that evening services would resume that night. "We've had him taken to Boston for treatment," Bishop John answered, when he was asked about Father Michael.

Brother Paul noticed Walter wasn't there and asked about him. A few Ways said they hadn't seen him since the day before. He also asked if anyone knew how to contact the members who regularly attend the services, but don't live in the commune. No one knew how to reach them. "They haven't been coming lately because Father Michael was too sick to be in charge. Walter didn't want to do it, so they just stopped coming," one young woman with a baby in her arms said.

"I'll go up to the house and talk to Hope. You two stay here and get to know these members. They're going to have to trust us," Bishop John advised the Brothers, as he left the barn. He let himself in through the back door of the Sutter house and found Hope in the kitchen. "We're very sorry about Father Michael," he said quietly, taking her hand. "He was a fine man and one of our best apostles. We don't think of him as being gone from us and you shouldn't either. He will always be with us, even though he has been elevated to The Greater Ways. It's the place we are all hoping to go after our work is finished here."

Hope shrugged and pulled her hand away. "That's hard for me to believe, but maybe that's why he looked like he was smiling when I found him."

Bishop John's face lit up. "Don't you see. That was his way of offering you comfort and hope. He was thinking of you."

Hope frowned. If Bishop John knew how she really felt or even possibly suspected how Michael died, he would be treating her very differently. So she murmured, "Maybe. I hope you're right."

"We're going to hold evening service tonight. We'll explain that we've decided to disband this Ways community and move everyone to other Ways locations. I hope you'll come and encourage everyone to make the move. Father Michael would count on you to do that," he said.

Hope shook her head. "This is my home. I'm not moving from here. I wouldn't be good at trying to convince others to move with you."

Hope's attitude annoyed Bishop John. "Where is Walter?" he snapped. "We need him to be a leader in the move. I want him to contact all the offsite members who might want to come with us. Father Michael told us that there are as many as two hundred who regularly come to the services.

Hope gripped the kitchen counter. "Walter is gone. He knows Michael is dead, and for him, so is Ways."

Bishop John glared at her. "Where is Father Michael's office?"

Hope showed him the little room at the top of the stairs and left him rummaging through the desk. She knew there was cash there and she wondered if he would leave some for her and the baby. And what about repaying Aunt Martha? She had allowed Michael and Ways to forego their rent over the last few months while he was sick. She went straight to Martha to let her know what was going on.

After an hour of searching, Bishop John went to the barn with a thick manila file. He handed it to Brother Phillip. "Get on the phone and call these Ways members. Let them know about tonight's services. Start with the ones Father Michael starred as having turned over their savings or committed to making monthly payments of one thousand dollars or more. They're the ones we want to convince to move to another commune location. Use Father Michael's office phone upstairs. Hope will show you."

Brother Phillip looked at the list. "Some of these people who are still working won't want to move. In fact everyone on this list may want all their money back!"

"We don't give money back. It's your job to convince them to come with us. Ways will take care of them," Bishop John insisted.

Brother Phillip looked worried, but he was afraid to disagree with the Bishop. So he nodded and agreed to do his best. "What about Hope?" he asked. "She should make some of these calls. They know her, and she could be very convincing."

Bishop John angrily shook his head and seethed, "Unfortunately, we can't depend on her. She says she's not coming with us. She is refusing to leave her home and her aunt. Except for the baby, she's of no use to us if she's not a believer. We'll come back for the baby after it's born. That child is Father Michael's and belongs to Ways."

◯

chapter 33

Martha was sitting in the solarium with her eyes closed. When Hope touched her on the shoulder, she jumped and stared at her. "The men you met from Boston are here again," Hope signed. "They 're telling Ways members Michael has been taken away for treatment and he won't be coming back. They're holding a big evening service tonight so they can tell everyone at once they are being moved to one of their other communes. This one is being shut down."

"When will everyone be gone?" Martha signed

"Soon," Hope answered.

"The end of Michael's lease is in August, and they should pay us all that rent that is due as well as for the past few months that he wasn't able to pay, including the utilities, "Martha signed.

Hope laughed. "Do you really think they'll agree to that?"

"We're not a charity!" Martha angrily signed.

The sound of loud knocking made Hope jump up. "Someone's at the door. I'll come back later," she hurriedly signed.

Officer Williams, Detective Moore, and a gray haired woman dressed in a navy business suit were standing on the porch when Hope opened the Medusa. "Afternoon Mrs. Brown, we need to talk to you again," he said.

Hope cringed and opened the door.

"This is Amy Tate from the Oakton Social Services. I believe you spoke to her earlier," he said.

Amy shook Hope's hand. "As I told you on the phone, we have a report from Officer Williams and Detective Moore that there may be children living on the property who aren't attending school."

"We have a few people living here temporarily. They're with a group called Ways, but they're going to be moving on very soon. The only children I know of are babies and toddlers," Hope explained.

"How's Father Michael?" Officer Williams interrupted.

Hope looked down. "He's very sick. The Ways Elders have taken him back to Boston for treatment."

"I'm sorry to hear that. Who's in charge of the group now?" he asked.

Hope shrugged. "I'm not sure. Some of The Boston Ways Elders are out in the barn now. You should talk to them."

"Are the children in the barn too?" Amy asked.

Hope nodded. "They're either there or in the outbuildings where the families are staying."

"Thank you Mrs. Brown. We'll go visit them," Detective Moore smiled.

The barn was filled with boisterous laughing and talking and hectic activity. Men were setting up extra chairs and benches, and the women were rushing to prepare tables of food and beverages. Amy and the two men stood in the barn doorway absorbing the excitement of an anticipated charismatic preaching mission.

Brother Paul noticed them and went to greet them and

extend his hand in friendship. "Are you here for the evening service? It won't be starting for a few hours," he smiled.

Detective Moore introduced himself, Officer Williams and Amy. "Miss Tate is from Oakton Social Services. There's been a report that there may be children living here who aren't attending school. She asked us to come with her to follow up."

Brother Paul frowned. "I'm new here myself, and I don't know the ages of any of the children. Let me find Bishop John. He's just taken charge of this community. Maybe he can help you."

While they were waiting, Amy moved through the crowded barn looking for children. She saw a few young ones playing with toys who she thought might be old enough for Kindergarten or First Grade, as well as several young mothers holding babies. She sat down next to one of the mothers who looked like she might be sixteen at the most and introduced herself. "What a beautiful baby," she said, smiling. "How old is she?"

"He's almost six months," she smiled back.

Amy laughed. "Well, he's going to be a fine boy. Is he your first baby?"

The girl tilted her head. "No, that's his sister over there looking at the books."

"Oh my! How old is she? Can she read?" Amy exclaimed.

The girl shook her head. "Not yet. She's just four, but some of the other girls are trying to teach her, and I read with her sometimes too."

Amy smiled again. "That's wonderful. I don't see any older children here. Are they in school?"

Before the girl could answer, Bishop John interrupted and

introduced himself. "Detective Moore tells me you have some questions."

Amy stood up to face him. "Yes, I do," she answered calmly, and then turned back and patted the young mother on the shoulder. "So nice talking to you, dear."

"I've told the Bishop why we're here, but he says he just arrived. He's planning to move these people out of Oakton shortly," Detective Moore explained.

"I personally haven't seen any children older than the ones you see here," Bishop John added.

Amy adjusted her wire rimmed glasses. "Well, that young mother with the baby can't be more than sixteen or seventeen and she says she has another child here who's four. She also says there are other girls here who help with the younger children."

Bishop John shrugged. "I wouldn't know."

"Mrs. Brown suggested there could be more children staying in the outbuildings. We need to take a look there," Officer Williams said.

"I'll come with you, but again I know nothing about the ages of people in this community. Father Michael was in charge here and enforced the guidelines," Bishop John emphasized, as they walked outside.

A girl, with long dark hair, dressed in faded jeans and a gray sweatshirt opened the door to the first outbuilding. When she saw the three strangers, she slammed the door shut, before any of them had a chance to speak. The Bishop knocked again and shouted, "Hello, I'm Bishop John from the Ways organization. Is your mother home?"

"No!" a small voice answered. "Go away! Father Michael says never talk to strangers!"

Bishop John lowered his voice. "That's a good rule, but I'm a friend of Father Michael's. He won't mind if you talk to me. Is there another adult at home we could talk to?"

"Mary Jo is here. I'll ask her."

While they waited, Amy asked, "How many families live in these two buildings?"

"There's probably three or four family sleeping rooms in each building. Ways is about communal living and sharing, not traditional single family housing," Bishop John explained.

"Interesting," Amy mused. "But you must realize this property is strictly zoned for single family living only."

"I don't know that," Bishop John said. "I'd have to check."

"We've already confirmed that with the zoning department," Detective Moore said.

"Then I suppose it's a good thing we're shutting this community down and moving these members away," Bishop John answered.

A heavily pregnant young girl with bright red, curly hair cracked open the door. "Can I help you?" she asked.

"You must be Mary Jo," Bishop John smiled and introduced himself and the others. "I'm a friend of Father Michael's, and he said it was all right for you to talk to us."

Mary Jo opened the door wider and motioned for them to come inside. The other girl was hovering in a small living room lined with worn brown couches. It was a clean space, but the air was heavy with the smell of urine. A child in a diaper and undershirt who looked to be about a year old was standing in a playpen. The sound of more than one baby crying was coming from the upstairs.

Amy stepped forward and smiled at the girls. "My goodness. This is a busy house. Are you two babysitting?"

"Sort of," Mary Jo answered shyly, pointing to the playpen. "I mean that's my son Bobby over there." She looked at the other girl. "Sissy's baby girl is upstairs crying and Mindy is working over at the barn. Her baby is up there crying too. Why are you here?"

Shocked, Amy took a moment to grasp the situation. All these babies with very young mothers was so terribly wrong. She glanced at Detective Moore and Officer Williams and then Bishop John who quickly looked away. "We're just here to check on how many school age children are living here. That's all," she said, softly.

Both girls giggled. "We're too busy here to go to school. We had to stop," Mary Jo said.

"Are your parents living here too?" Amy asked.

Both girls nodded."They're over at the barn working. We take care of the house and the babies," Mary Jo answered.

"And it looks like you're doing a wonderful job," Officer Williams complimented them. "I have a daughter about your age. I'm not sure she could do all of this."

Amy agreed. "Yes, it's a big responsibility. Do you mind if I ask you how old you are?"

Bishop John stepped between Amy and the girls. "Thank you girls. You don't need to answer that. Those babies upstairs need your attention. We'll be leaving now."

Furious with the Bishop's intervention, Amy stepped around him and moved closer to the girls. "I'm so glad to meet both of you. If you ever want to talk some more, call me anytime," she said handing them her business cards.

Both girls smiled and took the cards. No one had ever given them business cards. They stared wide-eyed at these strangers as they left. And just as the door was closing, Mary Jo proudly called out, "I'm sixteen and Sissy is fourteen."

Outside, Amy leaned against the side of the building. "There's so much wrong here. I don't know where to start." She turned to Detective Moore and Officer Williams. "The school issue is the least of it."

Detective Moore looked at Bishop John. "What do you have to say about this?"

"It's Father Michael you should be asking, not me. My job is to close down this community because he is no longer here. None of these people will be remaining here," he emphasized and walked away.

"Convenient isn't it? Father Michael Brown has been taken away and the only people in charge are here to close this community down. Apparently, according to them, they don't know anything about the day to day operations!" Officer Williams exclaimed.

Amy shook her head. "I don't believe them. There are children here having babies and working like slaves. How many more are there at their other communes like the girls we've just seen? And what about the boys? Are they being abused too?"

"We'll talk to the Captain when we get back. He's going to want to open a nationwide investigation into the whole Ways organization," Detective Moore assured her.

"I'll write up my report as soon as I get back to the office. You'll have it by tonight," Amy said.

()

chapter 34

Branch did his best studying for the end of the quarter exams late at night while Livy and Rory were sleeping. Their little cottage was completely quiet then. Even the deadbeats at the Broadway Hotel behind the house had finally stopped yelling and passed out.

When the rumbling of heavy vehicles pulling up the street started around 2:00 am, he was surprised and he opened the front door. One after another old Trailways buses were going up to the Sutter mansion. Ed Baker was standing on his sidewalk too, watching the procession. When he saw Branch on the porch, he walked over. "What do you think is going on up there?" he asked.

"They must be leaving," Branch whispered. Or maybe it's a field trip," he chuckled. "But seriously, why would they be going in the middle of the night?"

"Maybe they don't want to be seen leaving," Ed suggested.

Livy, wrapped in a blanket, stepped out on the porch next to Branch. "What's happening? All this noise woke me up."

"We don't know. All these buses are going up to the mansion." Branch said.

Livy frowned. "How many buses?"

"I counted eight after I got out here, but I probably missed seeing the first ones. Look they're lined up waiting to get up the driveway," Ed said.

"Maybe they're getting away from the police," Livy said.

Ed looked at Livy. "Why would you say that?"

"I went up to see Hope a few days ago and the police officers were there. She said they think someone from Ways broke into our house."

Ed snorted and shook his head. "I told them that when it first happened. It's taken them this long to figure it out for themselves!"

Livy yawned and patted Branch's arm. "It's too cold out here. I'm going back to bed. You can tell me what happens tomorrow."

"I might as well go back inside too," Ed said. "You gonna keep watching?"

Branch nodded. "I'm wide awake. I've been drinking coffee all night. I'll watch from inside and let you know if anything happens."

At around 4:00 am he heard the first bus leaving the Sutter driveway. Again he stepped out on the front porch and watched the procession gliding slowly, and now more quietly down the hill from the mansion. He could see heads bobbing in the seats and faces pressed against the windows on some of the vehicles as they made the turn onto Broadway. Other buses appeared to have no passengers. He guessed they were probably carrying equipment.

After the last bus passed the cottage, Branch stepped out into the street. For no reason he could later explain, he walked up the driveway toward the mansion. Midway up, he stopped. A motionless forlorn figure was standing just outside the front door under the porch light. Her long pale hair shimmered under the light. He assumed it must be Hope, but he couldn't be certain. Her body looked too thin and strangely statuesque. The back of her head was pressed against the Medusa head Livy had described. The snakes seemed to twine around her face as she stared into the darkness. Then she turned her head slightly, raised her hand and pointed her finger at him.

An overwhelming feeling of dread came over him, and even though the air was cold, he started sweating. He wanted to run, but his shoes felt stuck to the driveway and he couldn't move. For several excruciating minutes, he and the figure stood staring at each other, until she slowly turned away and disappeared inside. Branch kept watching the house as he backed down the driveway, but there was nothing to see except the stillness and the Medusa faithfully watching. Feeling foolish and relieved, he walked back to the cottage. Safe inside, he found both Livy and Rory sleeping soundly. In his mind, he went over the strange encounter and asked himself, "What was that all about? Who was that on the porch? If Hope was on one of the buses with Michael, then who was that woman and why did she make him feel so threatened and afraid?"

()

chapter 35

The next morning Hope signed to Martha, "They're gone. It's just the two of us again,"

"I thought so, but are you certain?" she asked.

"They loaded all of them and all their belongings into buses last night and drove away. Can you believe it!" Hope exclaimed. "I'll check the barn and the outbuildings today, but so far, it looks like everyone left."

"Where did they go?" Martha asked.

"Hope shook her head. "I don't know and I don't want to know. If the police come back, I can honestly say I have no idea where they went."

Martha frowned. "No one asked questions about Michael?"

"I told you. The Ways were told Father Michael had been taken to Boston for treatment. They believed that explanation. Our secret about his death will go with us to our graves. The strict rules of Ways are working in our favor. Members are forbidden to ask questions or seek anything, even medical help, from outsiders. If someone gets sick and dies, it was meant to be. That person's life goes on in another world. It's all part of Ways' grand plan."

Martha nodded, but didn't answer. Instead she waved

Hope away so she could be alone. She wondered if Hope would be strong enough to keep the secret. After all, she was young and had a long life stretching ahead of her. She herself, on the other hand, had lived too long past her time and she was impatiently waiting for her disappointing life to be over. For her there was no grand plan for life after death in another world.

Hope left Martha and went out to the barn. She stepped inside the big doors and stood staring at the rows of empty benches and bare tables facing nothing. The speaker's podium was gone, as well as the large pieces of the sound system and the stacks of Ways literature. The kitchen equipment and small refrigerators had been removed along with the children's toys and books. Upstairs, the loft was just a bare open space with light bulbs dangling from the rafters. All the curtains, cots and linens had been removed. Nothing was left to resemble any type of living quarters. Afraid of falling and being left alone with no one to help her and the unborn baby, she held tightly to the railing and gingerly climbed down the stairs and sat down on one of the benches to catch her breath. Without the Ways music and constant camaraderie, and most of all Michael's charisma, the big barn meeting house was a void signifying nothing.

Looking around at the empty space, she missed all the Sutter history that had been stored there. She had asked Michael what he had done with the old cars, the fancy buggy, the big sleigh, the antiques and trunks of memories. He said he had rented warehouse storage space where they would be safe. She had believed him then, but of course Aunt Martha had found out he was actually selling the family heirlooms. He hadn't understood the depth of her difficult, disturbed life, or how important the family memorabilia was to her. Ironically, her discovery about his actions pushed her over the edge and brought about the end for Father Michael Brown. Hope took a deep breath and wondered if the storage place ever existed, and if it did was anything left? If he had hidden the warehouse information in his desk, maybe she could recover whatever was left and bring it home.

Voices and footsteps interrupted her thinking. She looked toward the barn doors and saw Detectives Moore and Talbot, Officers Williams and Holmes with Amy Tate and several other policemen. "Hello Mrs. Brown," Officer Williams called. Sorry we surprised you. We knocked at the house, but no one answered."

Hope smiled and stood up. "My aunt is the only one up there and she, of course, wouldn't have heard you. I should be getting back to her now. Did you need to ask me something?"

"We're actually here to talk further with Bishop John and some of the other Ways," Detective Moore answered.

Officer Holmes had been looking around the barn. "Where is everyone, Mrs. Brown?" he shouted from the loft.

Hope sat back down on the bench. "They're gone. They left late last night on old Trailways buses."

Amy sat down next to her. "Are you feeling all right? You look awfully pale and tired. When is your baby due?"

Hope managed a trace of a smile. "The doctor says a few more weeks. I'm really fine. I just need to rest. I was up most of the night."

"You said they left on buses. Where were they going?" Detective Moore asked.

Hope sighed. "I really don't know. After I said I wasn't going with them, they stopped talking to me. I don't even know where Michael is. When the buses came, I watched from the upstairs window. The Ways were like sheep being herded onto the buses. The women were carrying the babies, and the children were dragging knapsacks and shopping bags. Most of the men were rushing to load equipment and small pieces of furniture and mattresses. As soon as the buses were packed, they pulled away into the night and disappeared."

"What time do you think they left?" he asked.

"I'm not sure. It was in the wee hours of the morning, 3:30 or 4:00 maybe. If you don't mind, I'm going back to the house. I'm tired and hungry. Stay here as long as you like, but there's not much to see now," Hope answered and excused herself.

"Let's check the outbuildings. Maybe someone stayed behind," Officer Williams suggested. But those buildings were vacant too, stripped of some of the furnishings and all personal items. "I was hoping those girls we met might have hidden and managed to stay behind," he said to Amy.

"Or maybe they slipped away into the woods, but I doubt it," Amy mused. "They appeared brainwashed about their lives in the commune. Day after day they were doing what was expected of them, being submissive to men, bearing children, cooking, and cleaning over and over again," she stopped and looked around. "Complete slaves, but in their minds they were just doing what they were expected to do."

"We waited too long. We could have helped the children and arrested all the rest of them," he lamented.

"It would take years of therapy to deprogram the children

and the innocent adults," Amy pointed out. "If given the chance, most of them would never be able to function and live productive lives in what we think of as normal contemporary society."

Officer Phillips and the other officers had been looking around the rest of the property. "There's no one here. Looks like they all got away," he said.

"We'll put out the information about the buses to the highway patrol. If they stayed in a caravan, someone might have noticed," Detective Moore said, as they walked back to their cars.

Amy paused in front of the house. "I'm going to check on Mrs. Brown. You go on ahead. I have my car."

Hope slid open the Medusa slot when Amy knocked. "Can I help you?"

"It's Amy Tate, Mrs. Brown. I just wanted to check on you and your aunt before I leave. I won't stay long."

Hope closed the slot and opened the door. Amy stepped inside the foyer and looked around. "This is such a beautiful old home," she said admiringly. "I've lived in Oakton most of my life, but I've never been up here."

Hope smiled and showed Amy into the dining room. "The Sutter family has always been very private. I'm just having some tea. Would you like some?"

Amy settled down at the table. "That would be lovely. Thank you." I was worried about you in the barn. You looked very pale and weak. I just wanted to be sure you were all right before I left."

Hope set out the silver tea service and poured Amy a cup. "I'm feeling better now. The last few days and nights have been very upsetting. I haven't had time to take care of myself. Now that Ways has moved out, I can think of myself and the baby."

Amy set down her cup. "What about your husband?"

"The Ways Elders took him away. He's been very sick. They're taking care of him now."

"What's the diagnosis?" Amy asked.

Hope shook her head. "We thought it was the flu, but he just kept getting worse instead of better. Ways don't believe in doctors. They take care of themselves and rely on natural cures. None of that worked for Michael. So they took him away."

Amy frowned. "I don't understand. You're his wife and you don't know where they've taken him?"

"No! and I don't want to know!" she answered, her voice trembling. "I was naive when I married him. I thought he loved me, but I found out he was already married to Ways and its communal living doctrines. Michael viewed all the Ways women and teenage girls as his sexual partners, even if they were married. I believe he fathered other children here besides this one," she said, rubbing her abdomen. "I hope he never comes back."

Amy shook her head and took Hope's hand. "I'm so sorry Mrs. Brown. Can I call you Hope? How are you going to manage this big place and take care of your aunt by yourself with a baby coming?"

Hope laughed softly. "Yes, please call me Hope. I've been managing things here for years. I think I'll be able to take care of a baby too."

"I'm sure you can, but newborns can be exhausting and time consuming. Maybe I can arrange some short term help through Social Services until you get used to being a mother. I understand your aunt, Miss Sutter, is deaf and an invalid. Is that right?"

Hope nodded. "Yes, and she isn't able to speak. We talk with sign language and she can read lips very well. She uses a wheelchair or a walker to get around, because she's very unsteady and has a balance problem."

"Could I meet her? I feel certain we could provide nurse's aide help for both of you. At the very least you wouldn't be alone," Amy offered.

"I don't know," Hope mumbled. Aunt Martha doesn't like strangers."

"Please let me try to at least meet her," she repeated. "She must have liked your Michael, and he was a stranger at first."

Hope sat quietly thinking about how attracted her aunt was to Michael at first. How she was convinced he was her fiancee back from the past. But all she said to Amy was, "Michael could be very charming and charismatic when he wanted to be. If you wait here, I'll ask her to see you."

Amy smiled and opened her purse. "Give her one of my cards if that will help."

Martha was in the solarium reading when Hope came in and handed her Amy's card. "There's a woman here who would like to meet you. She works for Oakton Social Services. She's offering to find a health aide who could help us out when the baby comes," she signed.

Martha stared at the card and signed, "Do you think we need help?"

Hope shrugged. "Now that we're alone again, I've been wondering how we're going to manage when the baby comes. I'll be in the hospital for at least a couple of days. What if there's a problem and it takes longer? You'll be here alone with no one to help. A nurse's aide could help you while I'm away and then she could help me with the baby when we come home from the hospital. It would just be for a little while until I get used to taking care of a baby. Please meet Amy. She's very nice and just wants to help us."

"All right," Martha signed. "But I'm doing this for you, not for me."

Hope hurried out to get Amy, before Martha could change her mind. "I'll have to interpret for you," she said, as she led her into the solarium. In the doorway, Amy stopped and gasped. She stood staring at the beautiful floor to ceiling tropical plants and flowers and the fragile woman seated in a wheelchair inside the greenery staring back at her. She was dressed in black with a white lace wrap around her shoulders. Her long white hair was held back by diamond studded combs and her thin fingers dripped with diamond and emerald rings.

Amy walked forward with Hope and held out her hand to Martha. "I'm Amy Tate. I work with Oakton Social Services," she said and Hope signed. "I'm so pleased to meet you Miss Sutter."

Martha shook her hand and pointed to a chair. After Amy sat down, she swept her hand around the solarium."This is the most amazing room I've ever seen. You must be a Master Gardener."

Martha smiled. "I've been working at it for years and years. I am one with the plants. They are my children. Why are you here?"

"I was actually here to check on the children in the commune, but it seems the whole group has moved on," Amy answered.

Martha frowned and looked at Hope. "What commune?"

"You know Aunt Martha—the Ways people Michael brought here," she signed back.

"I thought they worked for Michael," Martha angrily signed.

Hope nodded. "Some of them did, but now they're all gone."

Martha pointed at Amy. "Why are you here now in my house?"

Amy's face flushed bright red. "I was concerned about Hope and the baby and you too. Hope tells me her husband has been taken away for treatment and now you two are all alone in this big house."

"We've been taking care of each other for a long time. I'm glad Michael and his people are gone. We don't need extra help. Do we Hope?" Martha signed.

Hope sighed. "Maybe just for a few days when the baby comes," she answered.

Amy quickly agreed. "I wasn't suggesting a permanent arrangement. You and Hope could cancel the help at anytime."

Abruptly, Martha signed, "Thank you. Hope and I will decide if we want a nurse and we will hire one ourselves. She would work for us, not you or the town."

Amy stood up and looked at Hope. "Yes. I understand. Please let me know if you need my help."

Hope walked Amy to the front door. "Thank you for coming. I'm sorry my aunt was so difficult. I'll try to convince her we need some short term help."

Amy put her arm around Hope. "I left one of my cards on the dining room table. I can find a temporary aide for you. Just call me," she coaxed. As she walked to her car in the late afternoon sun, she wondered if she would ever hear from Hope. Martha Sutter was a bitter, elderly woman, but despite her frailties, it was obvious she controlled and frightened her niece. Amy worried that Hope would not be strong enough to convince her aunt that they desperately needed help.

()

Chapter 36

A few days later, Livy told Branch she was thinking of going up to the mansion to check on Hope. "Her due date must be very soon," she worried. "I know you need to go to the library, but can you stay home with Rory for a little while?" she asked.

Branch frowned. "Are you sure she's still up there? What if that wasn't Hope I saw on the porch after the buses left? What if she decided to leave with Michael on one of those buses."

Livy shook her head. "I can't imagine her leaving her aunt, but I guess I'll find out. We've been so busy with you finishing school and me quitting my job and arranging our move to Atlanta. I feel guilty that I haven't had time to be a friend to her."

When Branch had described to Livy his encounter with the eerie woman on the porch that night, they had agreed it must have been Hope. But if it was her, they were confused by her strange behavior. Amidst all the weird Ways happenings, Hope had seemed the most level headed and normal. "If she's still there, do me a favor and ask her if that was her watching me that night," Branch said.

Livy laughed. "And can I tell her how scared you were when you got home?"

Branch looked away from her. "You had to be there. It

wasn't funny at all."

Livy hugged him. "I'm sorry. I was just teasing you. I've been afraid here ever since we found out someone had been in this house while we were away at Christmas. And you have been strong for Rory and me. I promise I won't be gone long. You two can have fun watching cartoons!"

Hope opened the door when she saw Livy on the porch. She was dressed in a long blue silk robe loosely tied with a belt under her breasts. Her blonde hair was tied back with a satin ribbon and her face was glowing. She hugged Livy and pulled her inside.

Seeing her changed appearance, Livy smiled. "My goodness Hope, you look wonderful. You must be feeling well!"

"I'm so glad to see you. So much has changed here. I've wanted to call you, but I don't have your number," Hope said in a rush. "Come sit with me in the dining room."

"What's changed?" Livy asked.

"The best thing is Michael and the Ways are all gone and they're not ever coming back," Hope gushed.

"We wondered," Livy said. "Branch saw a lot of buses leaving your house in the middle of the night a couple of weeks ago. Were they getting away from the police because of our break-in?"

Hope laughed softly and shook her head. "I don't think it had anything to do with your break-in. Although, that's the reason the police came up here at first. They seemed to think one of the Ways members might have broken into the cottage. But no, Ways left because Social Services and the police found out about the children not going to school and about all the teenage mothers. I think all the adults and most of all Michael were about to be arrested for child abuse and sexual abuse."

Livy sat back stunned. "Did you know anything about child or sexual abuse?"

Hope looked down. "I never actually saw any abuse. But Michael practiced and enforced mind control and the communal sharing of everything including sexual partners in Ways. The young teenagers were part of the sexual sharing. It was obvious when the girls became pregnant." She stopped and rubbed her abdomen. "Besides this baby, I suspect he had other children here. And it was all done to perpetuate Ways as a viable social movement."

Livy's voice was hushed."I'm sorry. You don't have to answer this, but I have to ask. Are you sure Michael is your baby's father?"

Hope frowned and stared hard at Livy. "You have to believe me about this. I refused to take part in the Ways rule of sharing sexual partners. Michael and I fought about it all the time. This is his baby."

"I believe you, " Livy said. "When is Michael coming back?"

"I told you he's not coming back. "I'm having this baby alone, and it will be my child!" Hope snapped.

Livy stared at her and tried to think of a sensitive way to describe to her how hard having a baby is—not just physically, but mentally and emotionally. She couldn't imagine doing it alone without Branch. She reached across the table to take Hope's hand. "You're very brave, but trust me, you're going to need some help. We're only here for two more weeks. I've already quit my job. Branch has finished all his course work and taken a job in Atlanta. He'll continue writing his thesis from there. What can we do to help you before we leave?"

Hope's eyes filled with tears. "You're really leaving the cottage?"

Livy nodded. "Living here was always only a temporary arrangement for us. I thought you understood that. What can we do?" she asked again.

"Could you drive me to the hospital when the labor starts?" she asked quietly.

Livy smiled. "Of course I can, but what about helping you get set up here? Do you have a crib and all the baby supplies to get started? And what about your aunt? Who's going to look after her?"

Hope took a deep breath. "I don't have anything for the baby yet, but Aunt Martha has agreed we can hire a health aide to help both of us for a few weeks. The woman from Social Services who was here with the police said she could find someone. I just need to call her."

"That's great!" Livy exclaimed. "Call her right away. It might take some time to find the right person. But while that's happening, I'll help you with setting up a nursery. We'll need to do some shopping. Do you feel up to that?"

Hope smiled and nodded. "Thank you Livy. I'd like you to meet my aunt. I want her to know you'll be helping me. Wait here while I tell her about you."

"I'd like to meet her," Livy answered quietly.

Hope was back in a few minutes. "Aunt Martha wants to meet you. She's in her plant room. It's her favorite place. I'll have to interpret the sign language for you. Come with me," she said, leading Livy through the Victorian sitting room and past Martha's bed in the library to the solarium.

Wide-eyed, Livy took in all the old, elegant furnishings, signifying more than a century of wealthy and grand living. But the lush solarium took her breath away, and she stopped and stood still in the doorway. This was not an ordinary plant room as Hope had called it. This was a tropical sanctuary.

Hope went ahead of her and touched her aunt on the shoulder and then motioned to Livy to come in. "This is Livy Monroe, Aunt Martha. She and her husband and little girl have been living in the cottage since last August. She's offered to help me get ready for the baby," she signed and said.

Martha turned and inspected Livy and then motioned her to come closer. "So you're the one that's been living in my cottage?" she signed.

Livy smiled. "Yes, it's a beautiful house. I'm happy to meet you Miss Sutter."

"And you've offered to help Hope?" she signed.

"I'll do what I can," Livy said. "But we'll have to hurry. This baby will be here before she knows it."

Martha nodded and mouthed "GOOD" and then turned away.

Hope signed, "Thank you Aunt Martha," and walked Livy back to the foyer. "I'm sorry she seemed rude. It's not you at all. It's just her manner."

"It's fine. I don't mind," Livy said. "I'll go home and make a list of what we'll need to shop for. "She pulled out a notepad from her purse. "Here's my number. Call us anytime day or night when the labor pains start. Now give me your number and I'll call you about the shopping trip. Everything is going to be all right, but you must call about the nurse's aide right away. "

Hope thanked her again, closed the front door, and went back to Martha. "What did you think of Livy?" she signed.

"I'm glad you have a friend to help you. Just don't get too close with her and don't ever tell her what really happened to Michael," she warned.

Hope frowned. "Of course I won't tell her. Why would I do that? She's just going to help me get set up for the baby, and then she's going to take me to the hospital when it's time. That's all."

"You'll need cash for shopping. Take as much as you want out of the lock box. All of it will be yours and the baby's someday soon anyway," Martha signed back.

Hope hugged her. "Thank you Aunt Martha. This little person will be yours as much as mine."

○

chapter 37

Branch and Rory were in the kitchen making peanut butter sandwiches when Livy got home. "How'd it go?" he asked.

She kissed them both and sat down at the table. "Better than expected. Hope was there. She looks great and seems happy. She said Father Michael and Ways are gone for good and she's glad. Apparently their marriage is over," Livy explained.

"You mean he really chose Ways over his wife and child! How could he do that?" Branch exclaimed.

Livy sighed. "It wasn't your traditional marriage. There was a lot of sharing of sexual partners, including some of the young teenage girls. Hope thinks Father Michael fathered other babies in the commune. She's certain she's carrying his baby because she refused to have sexual relations with any of the other men. She said Father Michael was furious about that because it went against the rules of Ways."

"Did she explain why they picked up and left in the middle of the night?" he asked.

"Hope believes the police were about to charge Father Michael and the other adults with child abuse and maybe sexual abuse too. She thinks those suspicions got started when they went up to the barn to interview some of the Ways about our break-in. The police were pretty certain someone from the commune was responsible for that. That's when they saw some of the children," Livy said.

Branch chuckled. "That's pretty ironic. Father Michael tried so hard to convince us to join Ways, and of course we wouldn't. In the end it was the investigation into our break-in that eventually led to the whole Sutter Court Ways experiment going down!"

Livy pursed her lips. "There's something else I need to tell you. Hope asked me to drive her to the hospital when she goes into labor and I agreed. I also offered to help her set up a nursery for the baby. She hasn't done anything yet."

Branch frowned. "She really doesn't have anyone else who could help her?"

"No. She and Martha are up there alone. And that's another thing. Hope insisted on introducing me to Martha."

"Wow! You met the infamous Martha Sutter. What was she like?"

Livy shook her head. "I didn't know what to expect. She's elegantly old with long white hair and lots of sparkling diamonds. Hope interpreted our short conversation with sign language, and it was clear she wasn't very happy to meet me. All she said was 'Good' about me helping Hope with the baby. The most interesting thing was the solarium where she spends her days in her wheelchair. It's an amazing, exotic room, bursting with tropical plants and flowers. I've never seen anything like it. She's..."

Branch interrupted her. "She has long white hair! Is she really wheelchair bound? I mean can she stand or walk at all?"

Livy felt confused. "I don't know. Why are you asking?"

"Because maybe that's who I saw standing outside the front door with those snakes encircling her head after the buses left!" She was alone and no one helped her back inside. I'd feel better about Hope if it turned out to be Martha who gave me such a wicked feeling. Did you ask Hope if it was her?"

Livy shrugged. "No, but now that I've met Martha Sutter, I suppose I could ask Hope about that and the wheelchair use. I did notice her bed is set up downstairs in the library, so she probably can't climb stairs. Maybe she is able to walk, but the wheelchair just makes it easier for her to get around. I really don't think it's any of our business."

"You didn't see what I saw that night. It was pure evil," Branch sulked.

()

chapter 38

Over the next few days Livy and Hope dived into baby shopping. At first Hope was timid and claimed she only needed a few items, but after a few hours, the world of all things baby seduced her and she became excited about the enormity of having a baby. Each day they returned to the mansion with a carload of equipment, clothes, diapers, linens, bottles, pacifiers, formula and stuffed animals. Finally after unloading the last of the packages, Livy went home to ask Branch to set up the crib.

Exhausted, Hope lay down in the sitting room and began to read **The First Twelve Months**, a baby book, Livy had insisted she buy. Almost immediately she fell asleep with the book on her chest. The sound of the door knocker made her open her eyes, and she dragged herself off the settee and opened the front door.

Amy Tate smiled at Hope and introduced a pretty, young woman dressed in a starched dark blue Licensed Practical Nurse uniform. "This is Charlotte Tipton. I called you about her the other day. May we come in?"

Hope looked confused. "Oh Amy, I completely forgot you were coming by. Come in, "she said, shaking Charlotte's hand.

"How are you doing?" Amy asked cautiously. "You look tired."

Hope managed a smile. "I was just napping. A friend has been helping me with shopping and getting set up for the baby. We're almost finished. Her husband is coming over later to set up the crib."

"Maybe you could show Charlotte around the house so she can get a feel for things. And she should meet your aunt too," Amy suggested.

"I'll be happy to show you around the house, but Aunt Martha may not be up to meeting you just now. While I ask her, you could look at the kitchen and dining room," she said, pointing across the foyer.

Martha scowled at Hope when she hurried into the solarium. "What is it?" she signed.

"Amy Tate is here with the nurse. Would you mind meeting her?" Hope asked.

Martha shook her head. "I don't need a nurse."

"No. You don't need one now," Hope agreed. "But you will need help for a few days when the baby comes. She can fix your meals and help you with the bathroom and dressing. It will only be for a little while. Please at least meet her," Hope pleaded.

Martha turned away and didn't answer. So Hope decided to take a chance and bring Charlotte in anyway. "My aunt doesn't think she needs your help. You'll have to help me convince her. You do know how to sign, don't you? That might help."

Charlotte nodded. "I learned sign language when I was five years old. My little sister was born deaf. My whole family has been signing with her ever since. We're so used to it, we sign to each other sometimes, even when she's not around," she laughed softly.

Hope smiled. I've been signing all my life too. Both my

parents were deaf. My aunt taught me to talk, but then later in life she also became deaf from Meniere's disease."

"That's a terrible hereditary curse," Charlotte said. "I've read it drives some people out of their minds. And there's still no known cure. Are you worried about yourself and the baby?"

"It's on my mind all the time, but there's nothing I can do except pray that I'm not carrying it and it skips over both us," she sighed. "Come with me and let me try to introduce you to my aunt."

Charlotte and Amy followed Hope into the library first. "My aunt sleeps there," she said, pointing to the single bed. "Her bathroom with a raised toilet is in here," she said, opening two double doors. "There's a walk-in shower with a seat which she can manage herself, but she still usually prefers for me to give her sponge baths. Don't try to help her with bathing unless she asks you for help. She'll be embarrassed and insulted. After she's cleaned up and dressed for the day, she uses the wheelchair to move around this room and the solarium where she usually stays all day," she finished, opening the French doors.

Guessing that Hope would force Amy and the nurse on her, Martha had wheeled herself into the wall of plants. She sat staring out at them through the ferns when they walked in. Hope saw her right away, but the other two didn't notice her until Hope pointed. "She's over there disguising herself in the plants."

Both women smiled nervously and Charlotte quickly signed and said. "Hello Miss Sutter. I'm Charlotte Tipton. It's a pleasure to meet you." She touched Amy's shoulder. "Miss Tate recommended me to help you and Hope around the house for a little while."

Martha looked her up and down, noting her professional uniform. "Are you a nurse or a housekeeper?" she signed.

"I'm a Licensed Practical Nurse. That means I can help you and Hope with medical or hygiene issues, as well as other needs you may have. "

"Hope prepares my meals. Can you do that?" Martha signed.

Charlotte smiled. "Of course. You just make a list of what you like and I'll follow it."

"How much do you charge?" Martha asked.

"Usually ten dollars per hour, but we could talk about a weekly rate since I will need to live here for a few days," Charlotte signed.

Martha frowned. "That's a lot of money since I don't need you."

"Please Aunt Martha, let's try working with Charlotte. She understands this won't be permanent," Hope signed.

Martha sniffed. "All right. You work out the wage and the hours with her since you're so set on this," she signed to Hope and then turned to Charlotte. "But if I don't want you to help me, you must respect my wishes and leave me alone. You understand?"

"Of course," Charlotte smiled and signed back, but Martha turned away and dismissed them with the back of her hand.

"I think that went pretty well, but this won't be easy," Amy said, as they walked back through the library. "What do you think Charlotte?"

Charlotte looked at Hope. "I'm willing to try if you are."

"Thank you Charlotte. Yes, let's try. Let me show you the upstairs."

After touring the upstairs, the three women sat in the dining room and worked out a weekly payment schedule for Charlotte. She agreed to move into one of the upstairs rooms by the end of the week and stay as long as she was needed—or wanted.

()

Chapter 39

The next morning Livy, Branch and Rory arrived at the Sutter house to set up the crib. "It's easier and faster for two people to put the crib together," Livy explained to Hope. "We had to bring Rory with us, but she won't be any trouble I promise."

Hope laughed. "It's fine. I don't mind. Sometimes the young Ways children came here to eat. They were always fun to have around." She stroked Rory's head. "Would you like a cookie, sweetheart?"

Rory shyly moved away from Hope and leaned on her mother's leg. "It's all right Rory. Would you like a cookie?" Livy repeated and Rory nodded.

"You go on up to the nursery and get started while I get the cookie," Hope suggested.

Branch carried the heavy crib box up the winding staircase. "This is a grand old house," he panted when they reached the second floor. Which room is the nursery?" Livy led him down the hall to a small room next to the master bedroom and they got to work unpacking the crib and laying out the pieces. Rory happily played with the new baby toys and stuffed animals.

"I could never have done this by myself," Hope gasped, when

she saw all the crib parts scattered on the floor. "I had no idea! Thank you for doing this," she said, handing Rory the cookie."

"It hasn't been that long since we did this for Rory. Hopefully it'll be easier this time. I need to get my tools out of the car and I'll bring up the mattress too," Branch said, on his way down the hallway.

Livy looked around the room. "You're going to need a rocking chair. You could put it over there in the corner. Are there any up here?"

Hope frowned. "I don't know, but I'll look around. There used to be a lot of old furniture in the barn, but Michael said he put it all in storage. Aunt Martha and I think he really sold it for money for Ways."

Livy stared at her. "That's very sad if he did that. I'm sorry I made you think about it. Don't worry. Rocking chairs aren't that expensive. We can just buy a new one."

After two hours of trial and error assembling and a lot of sweating and cursing, Branch finished the crib and put the mattress in. Livy had already taken Rory home after she started getting bored and cranky. "Now all you have to do is put on the mattress pad and sheet and tie the bumper around the sides. Then you'll be all set," Branch smiled at Hope.

Hope ran her hands over the crib. "It's beautiful. I never thought I would ever have a baby. This all seems like a dream. It's the one thing I have Michael to thank for."

"Maybe he'll come back, Hope. This is his child too," Branch offered.

Hope's voice hardened. "He's gone and he's not coming back ever. I am certain of it. He's not part of this life anymore.

I've taken care of that."

Branch was surprised at her coldness and the finality of her words. He quietly packed up his tools and walked toward the stairs. He paused at Father Michael's office and looked out the window. The view of the cottage was unobstructed. He wondered how many times Father Michael and Hope had been watching them come and go, or noting when the lights were on at night. When he turned around, Hope was staring at him with a tiny knowing smile, but when she spoke, her tone had a hard, mocking edge. "It's a wonderful view isn't Branch. Imagine what it was like when the cottage was the only other house in sight. All the rest were hills and trees, as far as you could see. That's what my aunt remembers. I wish it was still like that, don't you? Then maybe you and Livy wouldn't want to leave us."

Branch felt the hair on the back of his neck rising. Hope had suddenly turned sinister and dark. All he wanted to do was get far away with Livy and Rory. "Good luck with the baby Hope," he said, as he hurried down the stairs and out the door to the car. He could feel her watching him from that upstairs window and he had the same eerie feeling he had the night of the buses. He turned and waved to her, but she didn't wave back.

"Hope is very strange," Branch said to Livy when he got home. "It's like she's part of another world."

Livy frowned. "Did something happen after I left?"

"Not really. She was talking about how she had Father Michael to thank for the baby she thought she would never have. When I suggested that maybe he would come back, she got angry. She said he wasn't part of this life anymore and she had made certain of that."

"What did she mean by that!" Livy exclaimed.

"I don't know, but it sounded very final. After that, her whole attitude toward me changed. I left as fast as I could, and she kept staring at me from that upstairs window. I had that same terrible feeling from that other night. Promise me you and Rory won't spend any more time with her."

Livy smiled. "We're moving, remember? The only thing I have to do for her is drive her to the hospital if the baby comes before we leave. She and Martha are hiring a nurse to work with them, so I won't be needed."

"I feel sorry for that nurse. She has no idea what she's getting into," Branch murmured.

()

chapter 40

Two days later Charlotte moved into the house and began helping Hope with the daily routine of waiting on Martha. For her part, Martha wore a permanent scowl, but allowed Charlotte to help her as needed. She didn't complain about her cooking or her efforts to help with personal hygiene, but in every other way, she ignored the young nurse and pretended she wasn't there.

Hope, on the other hand, loved having Charlotte help out with all the housework and grocery shopping, but mostly she enjoyed having someone else to talk to. It was Charlotte who climbed up into the attic and found the antique cane back rocking chair. She dragged it down the old winding staircase and cleaned it up. "It's perfect," Hope glowed. "You're very brave to go up there by yourself. I never go there. I'm afraid of too many spirits from the past lurking around."

Charlotte shrugged. "There's nothing to be afraid of up there, just a lot of old stuff covered in dust, waiting to be found."

Hope sat down in the chair, closed her eyes and began rocking. The easy back and forth motion was soothing, and she thought to herself, "I can do this."

A week later around midnight, Hope's contractions started.

At first they were far apart and she didn't feel worried, but she woke Charlotte because she didn't want to be alone. Charlotte began timing the contractions and told Hope to call Livy as planned.

Branch answered and woke Livy who jumped up and took the phone. "Don't worry Hope. I'll be there in a few minutes," she said and hurriedly got dressed.

Charlotte was watching for Livy's car. When she saw her pulling up the driveway, she opened the front door and stepped out. "I'm Charlotte, Hope and Miss Sutter's nurse. You must be Livy."

Livy smiled. "Yes. I'm glad you're here. How far along is she?"

"The contractions are about fifteen to twenty minutes apart. You should have plenty of time to get her to the hospital. Wait in the car while, I bring her downstairs," Charlotte said.

Livy kept the car running while Charlotte brought Hope outside and helped her into the car and patted her hand. "You'll do fine. Just keep doing the breathing exercises we practiced," she said, closing the car door.

Livy carefully drove down the steep driveway onto Sutter Court. The hospital was only a few short blocks away. She parked at the emergency room entrance and helped Hope inside. The nurse at the desk verified Hope's preregistration information, phoned her doctor and called for a wheelchair. Hope collapsed into the chair and gripped the arm rungs when another contraction started.

Livy turned to the nurse. "The last contraction in the car was about ten minutes ago. They're getting closer."

The nurse nodded. "The doctor is on his way. We'll get her upstairs to maternity. Is the father coming?"

Livy shook her head and Hope panted, "He won't be

coming. I already wrote that down."

The nurse looked at Livy. "Will you be coming up with us then?"

Before Livy could answer, Hope yelled, "She won't be staying. I'm by myself!"

"Are you sure?" Livy asked.

Hope nodded. "I'll call you," she gasped and doubled over in pain, as the nurse pushed the wheelchair to the elevator and the doors opened and closed.

Alone, Livy stood looking around the empty emergency room. She felt sad and helpless. "I've done all I can," she kept telling herself and went to the car.

Branch was waiting up for her when she got home. He hugged her and asked what happened. Livy sat down on the couch. "Nothing," she said. "I took her to the emergency room and then she told me to leave. She's determined to have this baby without any help except for the doctor. She said she'd call me, and then she and the nurse disappeared into the elevator. So I left and came home. It was as if I was just a random taxi driver who gave her a ride."

Branch put his arm around her. "You were a friend to her and you did what she asked. Don't feel bad."

"I wish we knew how to get in touch with Father Michael. He should be here for her and the baby," she sighed.

"If she wanted him here, she could have tried to find him. Clearly, she does not. Besides, he knows where she is, so he could show up at anytime if he wanted to. You have to let this go," he pleaded.

Livy nodded, but didn't answer. She knew he was right. They

had to put this entire cult-like commune experience behind them. Ways, Father Michael, Hope, Miss Sutter, this sweet cottage, the cemetery scare, the break-in and the police were all part of a strange, surreal chapter in their lives that was closing. Ahead of them was a new life in Atlanta.

()

chapter 41

Two days later the movers were packing up the cottage. The process was going slowly, mostly because Rory kept taking things out of the boxes as soon as the movers put them in. There had been no call from Hope, and Livy worried something had gone wrong with the baby, but she had had no time to call the Sutter house and check with the nurse. Finally, around dinner time after the packers left, Branch and Rory went to pick up McDonald's, while Livy hurried up to the mansion to find out what was happening.

Charlotte answered the door and recognized Livy. "Hope is still in the hospital," she said right away.

"Is everything all right?" Livy asked quietly.

Charlotte nodded. "I think it is now. She had a long difficult labor. They ended up doing a Caesarian."

"And the baby?" Livy whispered.

Charlotte smiled. "It's a girl and she seems to be fine. They'll be home in a few days. After you left for the hospital, I called Amy Tate. She's been checking on them and calling Miss Sutter every few hours."

"That's wonderful. I'm glad someone is there for Hope. How are things going here with Miss Sutter?"

"She's difficult, but we're getting by. She really brightened up when she heard Hope had a baby girl. Now she's acting like a grandmother and talking about the future of the Sutter family. It seems to suit her just fine."

"Please tell her I said hello and congratulations," Livy said. "Our movers are packing up the truck tomorrow, and we'll be leaving the area. I'm sorry I won't get a chance to see Hope and the baby. Please give her this card. It's our new address in Atlanta. We don't have a phone there yet, but I'll try to call her after we're settled."

Charlotte looked at the card. "I'll tell her you stopped by."

Livy took her hand. "I'm so glad you're here, Charlotte. Take care of everyone. It's a big job."

After Charlotte nodded and closed the door, Livy stood staring at the Medusa head and remembered her first shocked reaction. Now she viewed it differently. As she ran her hand over the silver face and snakes, she felt an odd sense of strength and relief. Good people—Charlotte and Amy Tate—were looking after Miss Sutter, Hope and her new little girl. She understood Martha Sutter's idea of using the Medusa to frighten people away and she hoped it would continue to work. She dropped her hand and whispered, "Good-bye. Don't let Father Michael or any of those Ways people back into this house!"

()

chapter 42

More than a month had passed since Branch and Livy and Rory had moved into their new home in Atlanta. In contrast to Sutter Court, this neighborhood was filled with young professional families with children all living seemingly normal lives. They laughingly called their Oakton cottage their "AWAYS Home." Branch had settled into his new day job as an investment banker, and at night he worked on his thesis. Livy had found a summer program for Rory and a nursery school for the fall. She, herself , was planning to take the law boards and then apply to law school.

Their whole Sutter Court experience was quickly receding into a welcome distant past. And then Hope's letter arrived. It was oddly sealed with a round wax impression of the Medusa head. Livy couldn't decide if the seal signified an invitation to open or a warning of what was inside. Either way, her curiosity won and she carefully opened the envelope without disturbing the seal. On creamy Crane stationery engraved with the letter **S** at the top, Hope wrote:

Dear Livy,

I want to thank you for being a dear friend. I know you came to the house to see how I was doing and to say good-bye before you left. I think of you often and I have a surprise for you. I named my little girl Martha Olivia Sutter. I'm calling her Olivia for you. She is a beautiful, happy, healthy baby and she has breathed new life into this old sad house. Aunt Martha is a changed person, so happy to be a "Grandmother." Charlotte is still with us and we hope she never leaves. She takes care of all of us and manages the house for me. We are so lucky to have her.

I don't know if you ever met Walter Kelly. He used to live here with Ways. He was well educated and very dependable and became Michael's assistant. When Michael got sick, Walter tried to keep Ways going for a while, but when the commune started to fall apart, he left. I always liked him and I missed him. A few days after I got home from the hospital, he came back. It was like a miracle! He's not part of Ways anymore and we've hired him to manage our property. Despite my miserable experience with Michael and Ways and my overall distrust of men, I am happy Walter came back to us. He's a comfort to have around, and I trust him. Aunt Martha seems to like him too. He wants me to teach him how to sign so he can talk to her himself!

I want to apologize to you and Branch for something that happened months ago. It was Michael and me who spent a few nights in the cottage while you were gone. Michael knew that I still had a set of duplicate keys from when I lived there. He was very angry that the Bakers paid Aunt Martha cash for the cottage before he could get the money together to buy it for Ways. And then you and Branch refused his invitations to become part of Ways. For spite, he convinced me to help him scare you away from the cottage by spending a few nights there while you were gone. We messed up the house and went through your things and left those dead animals on the porch. We never stole anything, but that's no excuse. Michael's idea was to force you to move out of the cottage and prevent the Bakers from renting it out again. Then he could buy it cheaply for Ways. It was a foolish disgraceful thing to do and I'm embarrassed to have been part of his scheme.

Ironically, our reckoning was your police investigation which eventually led to Ways' collapse. If Michael hadn't become so sick (and Aunt Martha and I are certain he's dead), he would surely have been arrested. I am truly sorry I hurt you and I hope you can find it in your heart to forgive me someday. If you come back to Oakton, please stop and see us and meet your namesake.

Fondly,

Hope

Livy read the letter twice and showed it to Branch when he came home from work. "So that's why Ways left in the middle of the night. They were running away from the police. Now it all makes sense," Branch said.

Livy shook her head. "We don't know if any of what she says is true. I'm more upset that it was Hope and Father Michael who broke into our house. They wanted to scare us away. We hadn't done anything to them."

"It's because we weren't like them and we didn't need them. I always thought it was one of the other Ways, not their leader. You were right about the duplicate keys, but we underestimated Father Michael's capacity to get what he wanted one way or another."

"I have another question," Livy said. "What does Hope mean that she and Martha are certain Michael is dead. How do they know? I thought he left with the buses, didn't you?"

"If he's dead, what if Hope and Martha know something about what caused his death or even worse had something to do with it?" Branch asked.

Livy shuddered. "I can't imagine it, but then why would they be certain?"

"Maybe he never left at all, and he's up there in that decrepit cemetery behind the house," Branch said.

"How can we be even thinking such terrible things? For the first time Hope and Martha sound happy. That little girl is offering them new life. Father Michael's controlling Ways rules are gone. If he's dead, I don't want to know how or why he died," Livy sighed.

Branch handed Livy the letter. "Are you going to answer this?"

Livy shook her head. "I don't think so. It's sweet she named her daughter after me. But no, I don't want to encourage more friendship. I hadn't thought much about Hope or anything that happened on Sutter Court lately. And it's better that way for us."

Branch took her hand. "Good. Let's agree to leave all of it in the past. We've moved on. We don't know what we don't know."

()

Chapter 43

Surprisingly, Walter was enjoying himself at the Sutter house without the presence of Father Michael. He had left because he felt he couldn't go on living there without him or the safety net of the Ways organization. Now he loved his job managing the property and keeping the old place running smoothly. He especially liked working closely with Charlotte. There was something seductive about the way she swished around the house in her blue nurse's uniform with the tight belt that accentuated her tiny waist and her dark hair in a tight bun. He found himself imagining how she looked without the uniform and her hair loose around her shoulders. He wondered how long he could control his growing attraction to her.

Of course, he had always admired Hope and the support she had given to Father Michael and Ways. Back then he could tell she was attracted to him, but now she seemed to want their relationship to be more than friendly. For him the feeling wasn't mutual and he kept his distance from her, especially because he wasn't certain what his new Ways responsibilities would be in the coming months.

Today was his day off and he walked into Oakton. The University campus was crowded with summer school students. He remembered his days there when he was taking classes and partying night and day. It had been easy to get hooked on alcohol and pot. He had stopped attending classes and instead spent hazy days and nights sitting around questioning the meaning of life and death in the off campus basement "coffee houses." Father Michael had found him there. They had spent hours talking and Father Michael had gradually convinced him Ways was the answer to the mysteries of life on earth and beyond. Father Michael and Ways became his salvation.

When he left the Sutter house after Father Michael died, he had gone straight to the bus station. His plan was to go to Nashville and ask his brother for help. Instead he kept hearing Bishop John's words, "Don't worry. We will take care of you my son." At the last minute, he had boarded a bus for Boston, not Nashville, and his life took another turn. Bishop John and the Elders welcomed him and began training him as one of the apostles. His first assignment was to go back to the Sutter house, ingratiate himself with Hope and Martha and earn their complete trust.

He found a phone booth outside the student center and made the call he knew Bishop John was waiting for. In a low voice he said, "They trust me completely. I have the run of the whole house and property. Father Michael's baby is healthy and happy. Her name is Olivia. What is it you want me to do?"

"When you think the time is right, you are to slip away with the baby and bring her home to us where she belongs," the Bishop directed.

Walter leaned against the side of the phone booth and took a deep breath to steady himself. It had never entered his mind that he would be asked to take Father Michael's baby. Hope and Olivia flashed through his mind and he wracked his brain for an excuse to delay the Ways assignment. Finally he said, "This will take some time. Hope is still breast feeding Olivia. When she switches her to a bottle, it will be easier for me to do what you are asking. I'm going to need a car and money for the trip."

"Call us when you're ready and we'll send you the money. We're depending on you, Father Walter," the Bishop said before the line went dead.

Oleander, *Nerium*

Finding Ways
by
Patricia McGrane

()

REFERENCES

4 Notorious Cults in American History, https://home.heinonline.org: 2023/10

Beasley, NJ, "*Meniere's Disease: Evolution of a Definition*," Beasley, National Institute of Health, 1996, https://pubmed.ncbi.nim.nih.gov.

Bulfinch's Mythology, The Age of Fable or Stories of Gods and Heroes, Doubleday & Company, Inc., 1948.

Characteristics of Cult Groups, http://www.icsahome.com.

Cult Classics: "*Tennessee Is a Longtime Haven for Unconventional Religious Groups*," Nashville Scene, https://www.nashvillescene.com, September 8, 2016

Cults in America, Google.com.

Cults in Tennessee, Google.com

Esaak, Shelley, "*History and Examples of Bas-Relief Sculptures*," thoughtco.com/bas-relief-183192, August 27, 2020.

Gray, Charlotte, "*A Voice of Her Own*," **After the Miracle** by Wallace, Max, The Wall Street Journal-Books, April 15-16, 2023.

Green, Dominic, "*The Road to Nowhere*," **Everyday Utopia** by Godsee, Kristen R., The Wall Street Journal-Books, July 15-16, 2023.

The Guardian, "*This Is a Cult: Inside the Shocking Story Of a Religious Cult*," https//www.theguardian.com, September 30, 2021.

Hamilton, Edith, **Mythology**, Little Brown & Company, 1940,1942. A Mentor Book , The New American Library, 1953.

History of Meniere's Disease, Google.com.

How Stuff Works, "*Oleander Is a Poisonous Plant, Not a Cure for Covid-19,*" https//home.howstuffworks.com..>House Plants, May 27,2024.

https://www.designbuildings.co.uk > wiki > Bas-relief.

https://en.wikipedia.org > wiki > Medusa.

https://www.worldhistory.org> Medusa, June 14, 2022.

"*Inside The Cult,*" Farley, Todd, The Sullivanians, by Stille, Alexander, New York Post-Postscript Books, August 6, 2023.

Kahn, Mattie, "*Sex and Violence,*" **An Assassin In Utopia, The True Story of a Nineteenth-Century Sex Cult and a President's Murder**, by Weis, Susan, New York Times Book Review, February 12, 2023.

Kode, Anna, "*Where Folks Believe Death Doesn't Exist,*" The New York Times-Real Estate, October 29, 2023.

Mar, Alex, "*Utopia Among the Brownstones,*" The Sullivanians by Stille, Alexander, The Wall Street Journal-Books, June 24-25, 2023.

National Institute of Health, "*What Is Meniere's Disease?*" https://www.nidcd.nih.gov>health>menieresdisease, August 15 2024.

Oleander, Google.com, "What is the myth of the Oleander?" https//www.oleander.org>Oleander-Library.

Peace Lily, Google.com.

Pierson, Melissa Holbrook, "*Into the Depths of Silence,*" Losing Music by Cotter, John, The Wall Street Journal-Books, April 8-9, 2023.

Reddit.r/Ask Historians, "*Why Were People in the 60's/70's Such Suckers for Cults?*" May 29, 2023, December 7, 2020.

Scalera, Sally, "*Pet Owners Beware: These plants can be hazardous if eaten by dogs, cats, horses,*" Gardening-FloridaToday.com, June 4, 2023.

Vincent, Isabel, "*Cult's New Life After Death,*" New York Post, July 10, 2022.

ACKNOWLEDGEMENTS

Special thanks to:

* Breakwater Design, LLC (bwdandc.com) for the elegant, transformative graphic design work, the tedious preparation of the book for publication, the website design and other marketing materials.

* The retired police detectives who patiently explained the various criminal investigation procedures in the book.

* My Mother Louise—who many years ago when I was upset, after tragedies struck close family friends—said to me, "No matter how well we think we know someone—we can never know what might be happening inside a home when the doors are closed and locked."

* My husband Myles and our daughters, Ryan, Annie and Kate and their families who inspire me with their patience, good humor and support for "my writing thing!"

* Lastly, to all my extended family, friends, readers, and followers both near and far who continue to encourage and make me smile by asking, "When is the next book coming out?"

()

OTHER BOOKS BY PATRICIA MCGRANE

Because of The Horses

Legacy of The Horses
...Spring 1865,
The Sequel to
Because of The Horses

patriciamcgrane.com

www.ingramcontent.com/pod-product-compliance
Lightning Source LLC
Chambersburg PA
CBHW070457120726
47910CB00003B/1060